At Virgin

The Queen's Gambit is Clear

ASHWANI KUMAR

BlueRose ONE
Stories Matter
NewDelhi • London

BLUEROSE PUBLISHERS
India | U.K.

For permissions requests or inquiries regarding this publication, please contact:

BLUEROSE PUBLISHERS
www.BlueRoseONE.com
info@bluerosepublishers.com
+91 8882 898 898
+4407342408967

ISBN: 978-93-6783-498-5

Cover design: Shubham Verma
Typesetting: Sagar

First Edition: March 2026

CONTENTS

Chapter - 1

THE ROOTS

"Gehna! You look so pretty." Words she had grown tired of hearing. Ever since she became the village sarpanch after her father's health—both mind and body—started to fail, compliments like these felt small compared to the huge responsibilities she now carried. She wasn't just her father's daughter anymore; she was now the one holding the village together.

"Oye, wear these bangles, and don't forget to smile. They're your family," her mother, Sheela, fussed over her while helping Gehna get ready for the festival. It didn't feel like preparation, more like a push to get her out of the house, even if just for a little while.

"My family?" Gehna said dryly as she stared at her reflection, still as her mother fixed her sari. "My family consists of four people. You, me, baapu, and that stupid brother of mine who's sitting behind the bars?"

"Your father lived for these people," her mother said softly, clearly tired. "He loved them. He cared for them."

"And now his clothes stink of alcohol, and his body's giving out. Things need to change."

"We're just trying to survive, Gehna. Your brother's in jail, and I don't need to explain that to anyone."

"Well, I'm still here... I guess." Gehna slipped on her shoes and stormed out, her steps echoing down the hallway. As she passed her father's room, the smell of liquor and the sound of his constant coughing hit her. She grimaced, pulling her dupatta over her nose, and walked out the door.

The dimly lit streets stretched ahead, bumpy and poorly built, mirroring the slow decline of the village where she had taken over the responsibilities after her brother's arrest, leading to father's increasing alcoholism. Her friends, lively and excited, talked about the mela—the rides, the fun, the festive mood—but Gehna barely listened. She sped up, her disinterest obvious, just wanting to get to the fair, do what was expected of her, and leave as soon as she could.

As she walked, the sounds of the village swirled around her: the faint tunes of a Kishore Kumar song playing on a radio, the creaky sound of a hand pump in the distance as someone struggled to draw water. Canals quietly flowed beside the street, and children, full of joy, rushed out of their homes, dressed up for the celebration. Behind them, parents followed, dutiful and tired, doing what was expected of them.

The festival had grown in importance over the years. It was the village's way of marking time, of holding onto tradition. "Happy New Year!" someone greeted her with a big smile as she entered, even though celebrating something like another day seemed ridiculous to her. Gehna wanted to ask, "What's so happy about it?" but she kept quiet. Small talk would only lead to a conversation she didn't have the time or patience for.

As they arrived at the mela, her friends buzzing with excitement, they slipped through the VIP entrance, greeted by a level of attention that left them flustered. But not Gehna. She stood still, her eyes scanning the brightly lit grounds. The lights seemed too bright, too flashy, in contrast to the darkness she had been carrying inside for a long time.

The fair was alive with energy—vendors loudly calling out to sell their goods, kids screaming in both fear and joy as rides spun them into the night sky. Gehna had one goal: make a quick appearance, just enough to be noticed, and then quietly leave.

As she walked through the crowd, eyes followed her, but Gehna kept her focus soft, not really looking at anyone. She moved through the crowd, detached from everything around her. Children ran up to touch her feet for blessings, while men let their gaze linger on her toned, athletic body. Her fame as a national-level wrestler made her stand out, her sun-kissed skin glowing under the neon lights. Even though she wished to blend in, the attention was unavoidable. Elders raised their hands in blessing as she passed, and she responded with a polite bow, folding her hands—an act that felt both powerful and forced.

These social duties wore her down. Being the village leader meant not just taking charge but also dealing with endless complaints, requests, and issues. Every second she spent here felt like a chore, a role she had no choice but to play. Meanwhile, her friends darted around, planning which ride to try next, throwing playful looks at the young men who was trailing behind them, flirting and whistling.

"Let's go," Gehna said firmly to her friends. "It's getting late."

"But we just got here!" one of them protested, casting another flirtatious glance toward the men, a small smile on her face as she waved at them.

"I'm leaving," Gehna repeated, her voice making it clear she wasn't going to argue. She started walking, her pace calm but steady. The men, sensing her seriousness, quickly turned their attention elsewhere, knowing it was better not to mess with her. Her friends, though disappointed, had no choice but to follow her lead.

Gehna had stopped caring about the social rules that tried to shape her life. Those same rules that gave her some freedom also came with their own restrictions, but she had learned to deal with them by not caring too much. She knew her friends weren't truly attached to her as a person; it was her power, her role as sarpanch, that kept them close. Their loyalty was fragile, more a result of her position than any real friendship.

As they walked back through the narrow streets, they spotted Chandu, the neighborhood boy who had always looked up to Gehna with fierce admiration. Kids like Chandu were caught between childhood and adulthood, eager to grow up but not fully understanding the responsibilities that came with it. He had started going down the wrong path—smoking hookah and chewing tobacco—but Gehna had stepped in, guiding him away from those bad habits and helping him find a better way. Seeing him out so late now caught her attention. It wasn't like him.

"Di...di... didi!" Chandu called out, his voice cracking as he ran toward her, pale and out of breath. He bent over, gasping for air, his words coming out in broken fragments.

"Dadda... blood..." he managed between heavy breaths, waving his hands frantically. He was clearly struggling to catch his breath, but the look in his eyes told Gehna that something was very wrong. She didn't push him for more, waiting for him to gather himself.

"Breathe, you idiot," she muttered, rubbing his back in calming circles, though her own heart had started to race with worry.

"Dadda is coughing blood," he finally whispered, his voice shaking with fear. "It's everywhere. He's not... he's not okay."

That was all she needed to hear. Chandu collapsed to the ground, exhausted and crying, but Gehna didn't stop to comfort him. Panic had already taken over. She turned and ran.

The village streets blurred as she sprinted, her sandals slapping against the dusty paths. She dodged through the crowd, barely aware of anything but the desperate need to reach her home. Suddenly, a family appeared in front of her. Gehna tried to move aside but accidentally ended up collided with a little girl, knocking her down. As Gehna hit the ground, she glanced back—the girl was crying over a fallen piece of jalebi, clutching it in her tiny hands. Gehna grimaced but didn't have time to apologize. She pushed herself up and kept running, her mind fixed on the crisis waiting at home.

When she reached her house, she didn't bother with the gate; she flung it open, sending it crashing against the wall. The sight that met her inside made her freeze.

Her father, Nandlal, once the respected leader of the village, now sat slumped in a chair, his frail body shaking with violent coughs. But it was the blood—so much blood—that made her stop. Dark red streaks stained the verandah, splattered on the walls, and soaked into the old carpet beneath his feet. The air, usually filled with the soft scent of her mother's incense from the home shrine, now reeked of blood, sickness, and a deep, suffocating musk.

Gehna had thought she was prepared for moments like this. She knew her father's health had been declining for a while and had braced herself for the worst. But this—this raw, brutal scene in front of her—was far worse than anything she had imagined. A knot formed in her stomach, and bile rose in her throat, but she couldn't afford to fall apart now.

Her father needed her.

Without hesitation, she rushed to him, her strong arms lifting his frail body as though he weighed nothing. She carried him to the car outside, each step feeling like an eternity as the weight of responsibility settled heavily on her shoulders. She had to act quickly. There was no time to think.

As the chaos swirled around her, she noticed her friends standing at the gate, unsure of what to do. She then glanced at her mother, whose face was full of terror—the same fear of losing yet another man in the family. Her mother, wiping her bloodied hands on the edge of her saree, had already resigned herself to the worst. But Gehna wasn't ready to give up. She couldn't bear the thought of losing another loved one.

“Take care of her,” Gehna instructed her friends, her voice tight with urgency. “And clean the blood from the floor.” She hated showing any vulnerability, but at that moment, she had no choice. The idea of leaving her mother alone in a house filled with blood was too much to handle.

Without lingering, she managed to get her father into the co-driver seat of the jeep, securing his seatbelt to keep him steady. She jumped into the driver’s seat, slammed the door, and started the engine. One hand gripped the steering wheel, while the other reached back to check on her father. She was racing against time, and every second counted.

“We’re here, we’re here!” she yelled at him, trying to get any kind of response, though her voice was filled with worry. Her father’s weak chuckle quickly turned into another fit of coughing.

“Hasse mat! Chupp karke leta reh. Aur aankhein bandh mat kare,” she snapped, fear creeping into her voice as she tightened her grip on the wheel. She bit her lip, fighting back tears, forcing herself to stay focused.

The jeep screeched to a stop in front of the only private clinic nearby. Gehna jumped out, shouting, “Doctor! O Doctor!”

The doctor rushed out, still chewing his dinner, but his attention shifted the moment he saw Gehna, drenched in blood from her neck down. Without a second thought, she grabbed him by the collar and dragged him toward the jeep.

“Do whatever it takes. I want my father healthy. Fix this,” she growled, her voice low but full of determination, enough to make the doctor spring into action. He climbed into the jeep, quickly checking her father’s pulse and listened to his chest.

But when the doctor realized who the patient was—sarpanch Nandlal—he swallowed hard, his expression suddenly changing. Something in his eyes shifted, and for the first time, even Gehna could sense the gravity of the situation.

“Say something,” Gehna snapped, her patience unraveling.

“His lungs are full of blood… or something,” the doctor stammered as he slid out of the jeep, “but we can’t treat him here.”

Gehna’s eyes flared with anger as she slapped the doctor. “Are you deaf? I said, make him better. You want money? I’ll give you whatever you need.” She yanked the keys from the ignition and threw them at the doctor, who barely dodged them. His face was going pale with fear.

“This is yours now,” she said coldly. “You’ll get more when he’s better. Now, work.”

The doctor trembled, shaking his head. “It’s not about the money. We don’t have the right equipment. We need machines—he has to go to the district hospital.”

His voice was soft, trying to calm her, but Gehna’s rage boiled over. She stepped closer, her eyes drilling into his, and snatched the keys off the ground.

“You’re coming with us.” she said, her voice icy, dragging the doctor into the driving seat, shutting the door in his face while shifting in the back seat holding her father. “Drive!” she snapped, glaring at the doctor as they sped off.

“Wait, Chaakan! Oxygen cylinder lekar aa.”

The doctor’s assistant rushed inside, finding an oxygen cylinder and mask kit and getting it to the doctor.

The dark, narrow roads stretched endlessly ahead as she weaved through villages, the blackness swallowing the path in front of her. Gehna turned on all the lights, trying to pierce the night, while her father’s coughing filled the jeep, the doctor holding onto the mask on his face. Every strained breath pushed her to drive faster, her heart thudding louder with every turn.

“Just a little more, Dad. We’re almost there,” she whispered, her voice shaky but determined as she finally hit the highway. The distant lights of the city flickered, and soon the towering hospital came into view, a beacon in the dark.

Gehna glanced in the rearview mirror and saw her father slump forward, his body collapsing against the seatbelt. Panic shot through her veins. Without thinking, she cut across a busy intersection, tires screeching as she swerved into the hospital's emergency entrance. She slammed the brakes, barely stopping before jumping out.

She rushed to the back and pulled her father into her arms, using every bit of her strength. The world blurred around her as she sprinted toward the emergency room, her breath ragged, her father limp against her. The doors flew open, and a doctor immediately sprang into action.

"Nurse! Wardboy! Get a stretcher—now! Prepare ICU room number 2!" the doctor's voice sliced through the chaos. In seconds, a stretcher arrived. Gehna gently laid her father down, her hands trembling as she brushed back his hair, still desperately hoping for a sign of life.

The doctor was already checking his pulse, his breathing, moving with tense urgency.

"Hurry!" he barked, as the wardboy rushed her father toward the ICU. Gehna stood frozen, watching them disappear down the hall, her chest tight and legs shaking from the adrenaline. The doctor shot her a brief glance, but no words were needed—he knew she was barely holding it together.

Finally alone for the first time in hours, Gehna reached for her phone, her fingers trembling. Twenty missed calls from her mother. She stared at the screen, her heart heavy, then put the phone away, unable to talk until she had something certain to say. All she had now was the gnawing uncertainty that tore at her from the inside.

Gehna sat down in the cold, sterile waiting area, her mind spinning. The chaos inside her had been constant ever since Chandu's frantic news, but now, it was starting to fade. Just as she was beginning to catch her breath, a piercing wail shattered the silence. The sound of someone sobbing uncontrollably echoed through the hospital halls.

Gehna froze, her heart pounding again. Instinctively, she pressed her hands over her ears, squeezing her eyes shut, trying to block out the sound. "Don't listen," she told herself. "Don't think about it." The screams felt like a bad sign, a sound she couldn't bear to process, couldn't let herself believe. Immediately, she stood up and stepped out, pulling out a pack of *beedi* from her side pocket and lighting one, taking a longer puff.

She needed hope. She needed quiet. Most of all, she needed her father to survive. But no matter how hard she tried to detach herself from everything around her, memories of another terrible day started to creep in.

—

Coming home from wrestling practice, drenched in sweat, Gehna rushed into the house, her throat dry with thirst. She grabbed a steel glass, filled it with cold water from the earthen pot, and drank quickly, feeling a moment of relief.

"Maa, I'm home. What's for lunch?" she called out, following the sound of temple bells coming from the prayer room. Just as she was about to step in, her mother's voice stopped her.

"Stop. How many times do I have to remind you? Don't enter the prayer room before taking a bath," Sheela said gently, without turning around. Gehna sighed, rolling her eyes as she turned toward her room. But then something caught her eye—a thin line of smoke drifting up from the rooftop stairs.

She had a hunch but wanted to be sure. And there it was—her brother, Deepak, who was supposed to be at school, smoking *ganja* with his friends on the roof.

"Oye!" she yelled, her voice sharp with anger. "What are you doing? What's that?" The smell hit her, and fury bubbled up inside her. Before Deepak could respond, Gehna stormed over, slapping him hard across the face, again and again, as his friends bolted, fleeing the scene.

"Why, Deepak? Do you think this is fun? Is this what you want to become?" she shouted, her voice filled with both anger and fear—the fear that her little brother was heading down a dangerous road.

The thudding sound of the door slamming still echoed in her mind. The loud banging on the door sent a ripple of tension through the house, and Gehna and Deepak both knew exactly who the police were there for.

"Kheda ke Sardaar, hamara pyaar bula raha hai, bahar aaiye! Kangan laaye hain thare vaaste!" Afzal Hussain's mocking voice rang out, his words laced with a cruel mix of sarcasm and authority. Afzal was just another corrupt cop, always chasing money and opportunities to rise through the ranks. But today, he wasn't after money—he was here for a much bigger prize: Gehna's brother.

—

The sound of footsteps brought her back to the present. She wasn't on the rooftop anymore; she was in the hospital, and a nurse was standing in front of her, tapping a pen against a clipboard.

"Please fill out this form," the nurse said, handing it to her before walking away. Gehna stared at the form, her eyes unfocused, before tossing it onto an empty chair nearby.

A few moments later, the doctor emerged from the ICU. Gehna rushed toward him, her voice shaking with hope and desperation. “Doctor, how is he? He’s okay, right? Please, tell me he’s fine.”

The doctor exhaled deeply. “He’s stable for now. He lost a lot of blood, and his body is very weak. He can’t handle any stress at the moment, so we need to let him rest for a few days. We’ll monitor him closely. Once we’re sure he’s stable, we can talk about a possible discharge.”

Gehna’s shoulders sagged with a mix of relief and exhaustion. Her father was still alive, but the battle wasn’t over yet.

Gehna’s heart sank at the words "for now." She had barely managed to keep herself composed until now, but hearing the uncertainty in the doctor’s voice caused the panic she had been suppressing to bubble to the surface.

“What do you mean ‘for now’?” she asked, her voice tight with fear, though she tried to control it.

The doctor sighed, knowing the gravity of what he was about to say. “Your father has kidney failure.” He paused, gauging her reaction. “On top of that, his liver has progressed from fatty to fibrosis, and it’s deteriorating quickly.”

Gehna felt the words crash down on her like a wave, knocking the wind out of her. She tried to steady herself, sitting back down in the plastic hospital chair, staring ahead as the doctor’s words rang in her ears. Her hands trembled, but she forced herself to keep a neutral expression, even as her mind screamed in denial. The doctor, noticing her state, gently placed the form in her lap.

“We need this information to proceed with his treatment. Can you fill this out?” His voice softened, sensing the burden weighing on her.

“I... I don’t know anything in English,” Gehna whispered, her voice shaky as she blinked away the tears threatening to spill.

Forcing a small, bitter smile, she added, "But I'm the sarpanch of this village. If that means anything."

The doctor nodded, sitting beside her again, understanding the weight of what she was carrying. "What's your father's name?" he asked gently, ready to help her complete the form.

"Nandlal," she replied, her voice hollow.

"And his occupation? Kaam kya karte hain?"

Gehna hesitated, her voice barely holding together as she replied, "All he can do now is live. That would be enough for all of us." Her facade broke, and the tears she had been holding back spilled over. She buried her face in her hands, her body shaking with grief. She had been holding it together for so long, for her mother, for her friends, for the village, but now the weight of it all was too much.

The doctor waited in silence, allowing her the moment to grieve. He completed the form with her as quickly as possible, but the emotional burden remained thick in the air, hanging over them both.

By this time, a huge crowd of villagers had gathered outside the house, their murmurs filling the evening air. Word had spread fast, as it always did in the village, and the people came—some out of concern, others out of curiosity. They filled the narrow street in front of the house, spilling onto the neighboring courtyards, waiting for any news of Nandlal.

Gehna stood at the door, her heart heavy with the weight of the moment. But when she saw the faces of the villagers—some anxious, some hopeful, some merely present to observe—she forced herself to rein in her emotions. The tumult inside her had to be tamed, at least for now. She could cry, break down, or even collapse later, but not here. Not in front of these people.

But she left out the part about the doctors' warnings. About the failing kidneys, the liver fibrosis, the slow decline that couldn't be stopped. The things that, if said aloud, would crush the fragile sense of hope she was struggling to maintain.

Her words carried a quiet authority, and the villagers, sensing her strength, slowly began to disperse. Some lingered to offer their well-wishes, while others made their way back home, satisfied with the news Gehna had given them.

—

Back at home, Sheela sat on the verandah floor, staring blankly at the bloodstains still streaked across the tiles. The image of Nandlal coughing up blood was seared into her mind. She kept glancing at her phone, desperate for any distraction, anything to pull her out of the darkness creeping in. Finally, when the phone rang, she snatched it up, her voice trembling.

"Hello, how's he?" she a sked, her heart clenching as she waited for Gehna's response.

"He's fine, Maa. They're keeping him for a few days because he lost a lot of blood," Gehna replied, her voice steady but carefully neutral, offering just enough reassurance to stop her mother from spiraling into panic.

Sheela let out a shaky breath, ending the call quickly before she allowed herself to break down. She buried her face in her saree, muffling her sobs as she shook, unwilling to let the silence of the house be interrupted by her grief.

Days passed in a strange limbo, with Sheela visiting the hospital daily. She found comfort in the routine, in the small, fragile moments of normalcy they shared during each visit. Nandlal seemed to be getting better—at least on the surface—and the family clung to those moments of laughter, of half-hearted jokes, of broken conversations. Yet, beneath it all, Gehna couldn't shake the dread gnawing at her. She knew what was coming, knew her father wasn't going to survive, but she kept that knowledge buried deep, refusing to tarnish the brief peace her parents had found.

One evening, they sat together in the hospital room, the news flickering on the television as Sheela peeled oranges for Nandlal. Gehna sat in silence, her thoughts distant, lost in the storm raging inside her. When the doctor entered, she snapped back to attention, quickly rising and catching him by the door before he could speak.

"He doesn't know," she said in a low voice, glancing back at her father. "Let's keep it that way, for now."

The doctor nodded, understanding her unspoken request, before stepping further into the room. Nandlal and Sheela exchanged puzzled glances, sensing the tension.

"I have the discharge papers," the doctor announced, his voice neutral. "You'll need to sign here, and then you're free to take him home."

Sheela's eyes lit up briefly, the idea of Nandlal returning home filling her with a fleeting sense of hope. Gehna, however, knew this was only a temporary reprieve, the shadow of what was to come never far from her thoughts.

Relief washed over Sheela's face as she hurriedly packed their belongings into worn, mismatched bags, their faded logos remnants of tobacco companies. It was as if packing up their things, the tangible act of leaving, somehow symbolized leaving behind the fear that had loomed over them in the hospital.

"Thank you, doctor," Gehna whispered as she passed the physician in the hallway. He gave her a brief, understanding nod in return, the kind doctors offer when they know there's little left to say, when all that can be done is left in the hands of fate.

"One last thing," the doctor said, turning to both Sheela and Gehna. "No more drinking or smoking. None. Under any circumstances. I'm counting on you to make sure he follows through." His gaze lingered on Gehna for a moment longer, knowing she was the one who could enforce that kind of discipline. They both nodded, bracing themselves for the responsibility of keeping Nandlal alive, knowing how fragile his body had become.

After the bags were packed, they exited the hospital to find a small crowd gathered outside—neighbors, distant relatives, and a few familiar faces from the village, eager to welcome Nandlal back. Their eyes were filled with concern, some with pity, others with hope. Gehna scanned the group, looking for the comforting presence of her friends, but they were nowhere to be seen. She knew, deep down, they were unlikely to show. Disappointment welled up briefly, but she tamped it down. Expecting less from others had always been her way of protecting herself, and so, once again, she let it go.

That evening, after the dust had settled and she had bathed, Gehna came downstairs for dinner, hoping for a few minutes of peace before the weight of everything crept back in. As she stepped into the dining room, the sight of her father sitting with a cigarette between his fingers while pouring whiskey stopped her cold. She felt her heart leap to her throat, her fury rising too quickly to contain.

"What are you doing?" she asked, her voice trembling with the effort to remain composed.

Nandlal, without even glancing up, replied, "Taking my medicines," his tone nonchalant, as if he were discussing the weather.

The calmness of his response only fueled the storm building inside Gehna. Without thinking, she stepped forward, snatching the cigarette from his hand and crushing it beneath her bare feet.

"That's not water," she demanded, her voice cracking. She wasn't just angry—she was desperate. She couldn't understand how, after everything, he could still be so careless.

Nandlal's answer came in disjointed fragments, each word heavy with bitterness. "What's the point?" He looked up at her, his eyes hollow. "Deepak's rotting in jail for ten more years. *Aur tu, beta, ek fal santra kharab hone se, saare phal fenk na diye jaanve hain. Dekh le ek do rishte aur, maan meri baat.* Look at me? I'm 60. What am I living for?"

Gehna's anger faltered for a moment, replaced by something softer, more raw. "What do you want?" she asked quietly, her voice stripped bare of anger. It was no longer a reprimand but a plea for some kind of understanding.

"I want my son back," Nandlal whispered, pulling another cigarette from his pocket. His hands shook slightly, but his resolve was clear.

Before he could light it, Gehna slapped it out of his hand, her frustration now boiling over. "You're dying," she hissed, her voice cracking. "Do you not get that?" Her breath hitched as she fought to keep the tears from falling. "I'm trying to save you, Baba. Don't you see that?"

Her words hung in the air like a heavy cloud, suffocating the room into silence. Sheela, who had been standing quietly near the kitchen doorway, froze, her eyes wide with shock, watching the confrontation unfold but unable to intervene. Nandlal, however, rose slowly from his chair, his frail body trembling, not with fear, but with anger and resignation.

"I'll do whatever you want. If you bring my son back," he repeated quietly, this time with more sorrow than bitterness. He turned his back to Gehna and walked away, retreating into the shadows of the house.

And in that moment, Gehna felt a crushing helplessness wash over her. No matter how hard she fought for her father's life, no matter how many battles she won against his illness, she couldn't give him the one thing he truly wanted—his son, her brother. The weight of it all settled heavily on her chest as she stood there, tears finally slipping down her face, knowing that some things were beyond saving.

Chapter - 2

BAD POWER

Sitting in a jail cell, Deepak reflected on the life he had lived and the moments when everything changed. How had he gone from being a boy trying to find his way to becoming an irredeemable criminal, now seen as a threat to society? The worst part was knowing that every decision he made had been made with a clear mind. There was no external force pushing him—his friends, the distance he created from his education, the drugs, the guns, the anger—it had all led him here.

It felt as if society had wiped him away like a stain, cleansing the streets of scum—those deemed dangerous and unhealthy to the system. And yet, even after everything he had done, Deepak had never imagined he would be considered part of that group.

"Namaskar saheb. Dal chawal kha loge, ya bakra katun?"

Deepak recognized the inspector from a past incident, and suddenly, the weight of the situation hit him harder.

“Eat fast, Afzal sir is waiting.”

The reality was inescapable now—he was caught. Not because the police had overwhelming evidence, but because Deepak had given up. The silence of the past few days had gnawed at him, and every minute felt heavier than the last. He stopped thinking and began to eat, taking such large bites that he hoped to choke himself, desperate to end it all. His family’s helpless faces flashed before him, and soon, he was sobbing uncontrollably between hiccups as he finished his meal.

"Nandlal parivar ke vaaris, aaiye!" Afzal's voice called out from the interrogation room. Deepak took a seat across from him. "So, where are your friends?" The question hit Deepak harder than he expected. *Where were they?* Not once had they come to see him in the last few days. He had expected at least that much.

"Raju! Where's my tea!" Afzal shouted, storming out of the room and leaving Deepak alone. Alone with his thoughts, and the rusted, corroded dishes of the jail—a stark reminder of the life he had lived until now.

—

The early years of schooling were shaped by a life of privilege. He grew up surrounded by fine things—eating from expensive cutlery, attending top-tier schools, and having his own library full of books. He spent his childhood reading the works of great poets and authors, with plenty of free time to explore ideas and form opinions about what was fair and unfair in the world.

Thanks to his father's influence over the region, Deepak had access to countless opportunities and resources. His presence was well-respected at school, and his popularity brought him into the company of a unique group of friends. They helped him navigate bullies and set him apart from other students. His closest friends were Raghu, Satyam, and Rocky—each one bringing something different to the group. Raghu always added excitement, Satyam was the thrill-seeker, and Rocky, older by three years, took charge of organizing everything, from plans to supplies.

All of them came from wealthy families whose lands had been sold to the government for large sums of money. Their families were influential in various powerful circles—connected to crime, land deals, security, and even contract killings. Deepak understood these were influential people, but he always felt a sense of superiority, knowing his father's status was even greater.

One day, like many before, the group was riding in Raghu's car, enjoying their usual routine. "Share the duties. I want a joint ready by the time we hit the petrol pump," Raghu said, tossing a packet of hash to the backseat. Satyam, lounging comfortably in the back, offered to help. "Hand me the paper, I'll clean."

But Raghu had a different plan this time. "No, let Deepak do it. It's time our friend gets the hang of our group's traditions." Deepak had smoked with them before, but this would be his first time rolling a joint himself.

Deepak spread the paper on his lap, staring at the piece of hash in his hand with uncertainty. Rocky handed him a lighter and gave instructions. "Light one end with the flame—let it burn a little, but don't overdo it. Then break it into small pieces and sprinkle it evenly on the paper. Not too much at once." Satyam, glued to his phone, barely paid attention, while Rocky closely watched Deepak's progress.

Raghu, seeing that no one was listening to him, lit a cigarette for himself, but Rocky quickly snatched it and gave it to Deepak. "Here, use this. Carefully light it, don't burn the paper, just keep it going." Deepak followed Rocky's lead, roasting the cigarette and then mixing its tobacco with the hash on the paper, crushing everything together.

Raghu was itching for a cigarette, but once he saw why Rocky had grabbed it, he refocused on driving. "Yeh le, roll kar," Rocky handed the crushed mix to Satyam, who quickly rolled a perfect joint.

"Deepak, light it up." Rocky was still unaware they had already reached the petrol pump, where two police gypsies were parked, one getting a puncture fixed. Deepak lit the joint and took a big puff, blowing the smoke out the window, right where two policemen were standing, wiping sweat from their foreheads.

The fear in Deepak's eyes instantly transferred to one of the policemen, Bhim singh, who burst out laughing. He could see a car full of kids—underage drivers, drugs, and minors.

"Bhaag saale!" Rocky shouted at the top of his lungs, and Raghu immediately shifted gears, speeding away from the scene. Deepak sat there, stunned, still holding the joint, while the others erupted in laughter.

"Bhenchod! Ghana chokha raad ho jaata abhi!" Raghu gasped, relieved as he checked if they were being followed. Just then, a police gypsy came storming out of the intersection ahead of them. Raghu quickly took a sharp right, pushing the car to its limit. Deepak, still shaken, took another quick puff and passed the joint to Rocky, who was now excited by the chase.

“Re faaltu petrol hai toh mhari bike mein dalwa de. Rok saale ko, dekhien zara, ghana baazigar hora hai,” Raghu muttered, stopping the car in the middle of the road as Bhim Singh caught up and blocked their path.

“Na jaare prabhu, kahin na jaare. Tum aao bahar,” Rocky said as he stepped out of the car, taking another puff.

“Char balak, license dikhao,” the policeman said, holding a worn-out challan book in his hand.

“Parichay toh le le, tu bhi ghana hi subedaar hora hai,” Rocky replied, turning to the car and pointing at each of his friends. "This is Satyam, the son of contractor and shooter Prakash ji. The driver? Your MLA Shekhar Chaturvedi’s son. And this here is Deepak bhaiya, son of Nandlal, the gram pradhan of Kheda." The policeman swallowed hard, realizing the trouble he’d be in if he arrested any of them.

"Saab, what should we do?" The sub-inspector, wiping sweat from his brow, saluted the boys as both he and the driver backed away and left.

"Arre, khaali haath kyun jaare ho? Do kash maarlo," Rocky called after them, laughing. It was at that moment Deepak truly realized the power he held over the law. There was no bigger drug than power and authority, and now Deepak understood that. This realization gave him a sense of liberation, more than a kid should ever feel.

“If you could get away with anything, what would you do?” Deepak had been toying with this question for some time, but now, with nothing to fear, he felt free to explore much bigger things than just doing drugs. He needed to find out where the limits really were.

After this, Deepak began skipping school more often. But despite his frequent absences, his grades never faltered. He continued to top the class, and the teachers and staff knew all too well about the antics of this privileged group. However, they feared speaking up, as reporting the boys could bring severe consequences upon themselves. School had become a playground for Raghu, Satyam, Rocky, and Deepak, and they exploited every opportunity.

They vandalized property, peed in fountains and water tanks, started fights with other gangs in the neighborhood, and caused regular disruptions in school. The school’s sense of order was hanging by a thread, and the principal finally decided to take action by sending letters to their parents, arranging a meeting to discuss the boys’ behavior.

As soon as they found out about the meeting, they stormed into the principal's office.

“May I come in, sir?” Deepak asked mockingly as they barged in. The principal, sitting with other headmasters over tea, immediately understood they were there to intimidate him.

"Have a seat, I’ll get you some tea," the principal said calmly, gesturing for the headmasters to leave. But Deepak, Satyam, and Raghu stayed put, holding their ground while Rocky stood behind the principal’s chair, gripping it firmly so the principal couldn’t see him.

"Did you send a love letter to my father?" Deepak asked coldly, pulling out the letter the principal had sent to his home, addressed to his father.

"Why didn't you ask?" Deepak snapped, slapping the principal hard across the face. "Did you ask any of us before sending it?"

Deepak picked up the letter and mockingly read aloud, "The school would like to inform you that your son, Deepak Singh, is terminated. We would like to discuss the reasons and solutions in person, and this is the reason I'm writing to you for..." He grabbed the principal by his shirt, yanked him out of his chair, and threw him to the floor.

"What do you want? Money? A donation?" Deepak sneered, pulling out bundles of cash and throwing them at the principal's face. "You should've just told me." He kicked the principal in the stomach, leaving him groaning in pain. "And if anyone asks you about this from now on, you say nothing." With that final threat, they left.

Shaken and beaten, the principal wasted no time. He called the police, and by the evening, all four of them—Deepak, Rocky, Satyam, and Raghu—were arrested and booked.

—

"Inspector saab, jaan do. Baalak hai sabre. Re na karenge fir, pinky promise sir ji. Please. Papaji ko pata lagya toh thare ko bhi kuttega mhare ko bhi," Satyam pleaded, pacing around the cell, desperate. His hands were twitching, restless with the need for a fix. It was clear that the situation was spiraling beyond their control.

"Sir ji, look, raat chadh gai hai. Ghar chalo roti raani aaj hamare yahan kar lena," Raghu tried to charm the inspector, hoping to find a way out. None of them wanted to face their parents. But as the door opened, they saw Nandlal, Deepak's father, walk in and take a seat.

"Oye, thara baapu aaya hai," Rocky teased, nudging Deepak. The others, still smirking, greeted Nandlal with a mock salutation, "Ram ram saheb."

They made light of the situation, mocking the system and the corrupt power dynamics, but the inspector didn't seem to mind. He showed no resentment, no regret, knowing the influence of a village headman like Nandlal was untouchable. Soon, all four boys were released from the jail. Deepak tried to hide in the back, avoiding his father's gaze, but when they stepped outside, he realized something strange—his father had already left.

As they stood alone outside the police station, Rocky laughed, "Nice. That's how heroes work. He came, he conquered, and left."

While the others laughed it off, Deepak felt uneasy. This wasn't what he had expected. If his father had yelled at him, slapped him, kicked him out, or even beaten him to a pulp, it would've made sense. Any kind of outburst would have felt more real. But this...this silent neglect? It was absurd. It stung deeper than any punishment could.

Still, Deepak looked at his friends. They were all he had now.

—

Pursuing his higher secondary studies, Deepak sat, watching his grades drop, but for once, he was ready to put in some effort among his classmates. The teachers, despite his reputation, genuinely hoped he would improve academically. They knew he was smart, yet Deepak couldn't help but resent the comments about his crowd—the group of friends seemingly set to derail his future.

After a major incident involving the headmaster, everyone, including the teachers and school staff, remained cautious. They all knew these kids were beyond their control.

"As long as no one's in real danger, keep others away from them. We've got no records of violence or worse on file. Just let them pass, graduate, and leave in a few years."

Following this direction, teachers even allowed cheating materials, providing all the academic support they could, so long as there was no trouble on school grounds.

Deepak avoided unnecessary fights, staying out of inter-school rivalries, leaving other kids to handle things. He didn't need violence to get a thrill—an occasional run-in with cops, a bit of aimless wandering, and a brush with drugs sufficed. Even the police seemed powerless to intervene.

Everyone seemed to be waiting for the day when these sheltered kids would cross an irredeemable line, a moment when detaining them would be inevitable, and even their families couldn't help.

The indifference from students, teachers, and staff frustrated Deepak and his friends, yet they also felt oddly freed by it. No one cared about the frequent scuffles with kids from other schools, and the headmaster hadn't said a word since the incident.

Despite his indifferent attitude, Deepak had dropped out of school, missing exams and failing because of poor attendance. He showed no remorse about how things had turned out, as if he'd already made his peace with it. Over time, he had carved out a reputation for himself—a reputation built on all the wrong reasons. At school, he had become a figure everyone knew but few dared to approach. He was the man, the myth, the legend—the one who somehow kept the whole system, and the unspoken hierarchy within it, in check.

—

With the wind so strong, the trees were bound to face the turbulence. That's what happened to Deepak and his friends. Carried by the wind of comfort and power, their hunger for drugs and pleasure became stronger. Deepak and his group had found a secluded spot bordered by fields and trees. Meant to be a warehouse, the place, with four walls and no roof, had become their hangout.

"Deepak!" yelled Satyam, arriving breathlessly on his bike as the others lounged on a cot, sharing joints and beers. "Deepak," he panted, struggling with the bike stand, "Arrey, teri maa bula rahi hai, teri behen ko ladke wale dekhne aaye hain."

Stunned, Deepak grabbed Satyam's bike keys and headed home. "Maa! O Maate!" he called, staggering through a garlanded entryway into a cleaned-up house. There was Gehna, beaming in a red outfit, light makeup glowing on her face.

"Oye hoye, katai chamak laag rahi hai chehre pe," Deepak said with a half-smile, his words slightly slurred. Gehna just rolled her eyes and pulled him upstairs to her messy room.

"So this is how I found out," he mumbled, collapsing onto her bed, clearly drunk. She looked at him, unimpressed. "This is why," she muttered, watching him realize he was wearing mismatched slippers, reeking of alcohol, his eyes bloodshot, with no idea where his bike even was.

"Niche na aaiyo," Gehna instructed, locking him in. "Chhod de, ghar pariwar sab kha javegi ye aadatein." Deepak stared blankly after her, overhearing his mother asking where he was, his father arriving just as the guests were settling in, and the scents of samosas, sweets, and soda bottles filling the air. He felt rooted in place, but it wasn't just the alcohol or his usual detachment; it was the pang of knowing he wasn't part of this big family moment. And yet, he knew it was out of his control.

Downstairs, cheerful chatter and laughter filled the house as the families settled into conversation, discussing next steps for the marriage. "Arrey, Ranjeet aur Gehna ko bhi toh sehmati len do," Sheela suggested brightly, passing a plate of biscuits to the guests.

"What's the need?" Ranjeet's father chuckled. "Dekho ji, apne humne maan li, toh baat pakki ho gai, bhatera time hai, aapas mein samajhte rahenge baalak zindagi bhar." An awkward silence followed, which Ranjeet's mother broke with a polite smile. "Still, let them get introduced at least." She gestured for Gehna and her son to have a private chat, and the two made their way up the stairs to her room.

As they neared her door, Gehna realized with a jolt that Deepak was inside, likely passed out by now, so they paused in the hallway, caught in the kind of awkwardness that hovers when two people barely know each other.

"So, what do you do?" Gehna broke the silence, determined to fill the air.

"I'm a senior producer at Capital News Channel," Ranjeet replied.

"Oh, nice...so what are your main responsibilities?" Gehna asked, genuinely curious. Since pursuing pro wrestling, she'd left behind the world of academics and formal careers that most people around her had chosen.

Their conversation was mostly small talk, an initial step toward getting comfortable, but Gehna could sense an uneasy tension building. Ranjeet's gaze seemed fixed somewhere below her face. She felt a prickling discomfort and couldn't ignore it anymore.

"Oye, nazrein upar," she said firmly, as Ranjeet snapped his head up, caught in the act. He quickly covered, "I'm sorry, it's just... your body's really something. I've seen you at the wrestling grounds." His comment brought back memories of other men who'd made similar, objectifying remarks. She recognized his face now—she'd seen him before, lurking around the grounds with those same eyes.

"No, I can't..." Gehna said sharply, realizing he was not someone she wanted any part of.

"*Arrey, mauj ho javegi teri, jo mann kare kariye. Bas byaah kar le. Tu mujhe khush rakhiye mein tanne,*" Ranjeet went on, moving his hand toward her waist, then trying to grope her.

Unbeknownst to them, Deepak was awake and listening. He peered through the crack in the door, taking in the scene with growing fury as Ranjeet's hand slipped lower, trying to reach for her chest. Deepak's jaw clenched, his eyes flashing with anger, but he stayed put as Gehna caught his eye, silently willing him not to intervene.

"Bhadwa saala!" Gehna hissed, slapping Ranjeet hard across the face, pushing him back, and storming downstairs. Deepak clenched his fists, trying to steady himself, when he overheard Ranjeet muttering under his breath, "Saali kutiya, tu mil mujhe."

Deepak's eyes narrowed. He knew what had to be done. For him, this man was already as good as dead.

Downstairs, voices roared in heated arguments as Sheela and Nandlal berated the guests. Insults flew back and forth, but it all eventually dissolved into silence. Gehna sat alone in the dining room, her mother beside her, quietly peeling apples. Upstairs, Deepak lay on Gehna's bedroom floor, trying to process the chaos that had unfolded. The house fell into an uneasy quiet, with everyone dealing with what had happened in their own way—by cooking, staying silent, or offering small gestures of comfort. But Deepak couldn't let go of one thing: Ranjeet, the man who had been welcomed into their home, celebrated by their family, only to turn around and try to harm his sister. The thought gnawed at him, though he held back from dragging any more conflict into the home.

It was a calm Saturday morning, and Deepak sat by his mother, spreading butter on toast, when Gehna burst through the door, wiping her face with her dupatta. Her tense expression made both Deepak and their mother exchange a look. "Tu yahin ruk," his mother whispered to Deepak as she went after Gehna into her room. But Deepak had had enough of following directions, so he crept upstairs and listened in.

"It was him, he… He came to my wrestling match and…" Gehna's voice broke as she finally let her tears out.

"Baapu ko bata diye. Karte hain kuch." Their mother tried to soothe her, but by then, Deepak was already out of the house.

Deepak grabbed his father's bike and sped away, holding his phone between his head and shoulder. "Oye, Satyam aur Rocky ko lekar wrestling point pe aao, jaldi!" Hanging up, he accelerated, reaching the wrestling grounds within minutes. The plan was simple: wait for the classes to end, find Ranjeet, and take care of things.

"Rehnpat marne hai ya saansein tod dein?" Rocky asked from behind the wheel, while Satyam and Raghu, seated in the back, rummaged for hockey sticks and chains under the seat.

"Bhenchod, chain se kaun maarta hai," Rocky muttered, unimpressed.

"Bhaiya, picture mein dekha tha, bhadiya chhale pad jaate hain," Satyam replied with a grin, before turning to Deepak, who was already fixed on the main gate. There, Ranjeet sat with his friends in a jeep, laughing and making comments at the girls leaving the training center.

Rocky climbed out of the car, sizing up the scene. "Teri behen yahi practice karti hai" he asked, and Deepak gave a curt nod.

"Aur yeh launde chhed rahe hain use," he confirmed, nodding again. "Bhadiya" With a grim smile, Rocky picked up a brick and hurled it with force at Ranjeet's jeep, striking the driver squarely in the head. The guy slumped over, blood trickling down his face. Unbothered, Deepak raised his hand in a mocking wave at Ranjeet and his friends, who were too stunned to react. One friend rushed to help the bleeding driver, while Ranjeet, furious, stormed out of the jeep with a couple of his other friends in tow.

He approached Deepak with a smug look, taunting him, "Teri behen chhed di kya maine, hain re launde?" He looked down at Deepak, confidence oozing from every pore.

Deepak didn't answer. Instead, he wound up and delivered a vicious punch to Ranjeet's gut, catching him off guard. Ranjeet was built tall and solid, experienced in more fights than he could count, and he recovered quickly, squaring off against Deepak. No one moved to break it up—Rocky, Satyam, and Raghu were holding back Ranjeet's friends, letting Deepak take on the fight. This wasn't their battle to join; Deepak had to see it through.

But Deepak, despite his raw fury, was young and no match for Ranjeet's size and strength. Ranjeet's hits came hard, each one drawing blood, bruising skin, and breaking flesh. Yet Deepak refused to back down, even as blood dripped down his lip. Ranjeet scoffed, "You should've aimed that brick at me, kid. You wasted it on the other idiot." He said as he spat on Deepak's swollen face, Deepak laid there enraged, growling staring at Ranjeet with his eyes filled with fury. He struggled to stand up but he found his friends also laying down on the floor, getting beaten to pulp. He sat there as Ranjeet and his friends left the scene, kicking their way out of the space.

Deepak steadied himself as he climbed into the car, gripping the door for support. He chuckled briefly when he realized he was seated in the passenger seat rather than the driver's, but before he could switch, Raghu slid into the driver's side, wiping blood from his nose. "Where to?" he asked, hands gripping the wheel as Rocky and Satyam settled in the back, tying cloths around their heads.

"Follow them," Deepak instructed, settling in as they tracked Ranjeet's car. It led them to a house; Ranjeet had gone home. Deepak watched until Ranjeet disappeared inside. "Hand me something," he muttered, gearing up for the confrontation that now felt inevitable. He knew Ranjeet would never change; he had to finish it here. Satyam handed him a *hansli*, a reaping hook. Deepak studied it, gripping the cold metal.

"Oye, nahin! Bhenchod!" Raghu hissed, paling. "That thing can kill! What the hell, Satyam?" he yelled. But by then, Deepak was already at Ranjeet's door, ringing the bell.

Ranjeet opened it, only to be met with a sharp hook plunging into his chest. He coughed, blood speckling Deepak's face as Deepak drove the hook down, slicing Ranjeet's torso open in one swift, brutal motion. Deepak held Ranjeet's face, his fingers hooked into his jaw. "Never touch my sister again." Without even looking down, he severed Ranjeet's hand. The man's eyes remained wide, staring blankly as life faded from them.

"Ranjeet!" Ranjeet's father shouted, stumbling into the room to find his son's lifeless body beneath Deepak, who stood slowly, wiping blood from his face. The father froze, his eyes widening in horror as Deepak approached. But he had no time to react before Deepak swung, striking him down.

"Deepak!" Rocky, Raghu, and Satyam burst through the door, recoiling at the carnage. None of them had seen this side of him, and the calm way he wiped his hands was chilling. "Deepak!" Raghu shouted, tears filling his eyes as Deepak approached Ranjeet's father once more, preparing to strike.

Just then, Ranjeet's mother emerged, wailing and screaming. Sensing what Deepak might do, Rocky lunged at him, grappling him down, while the others rushed in to help.

"Aunty ji, namaste," Deepak chuckled as his friends dragged him out, wiping his hands on his shirt, eerily calm amidst the chaos, blood pooling by the doorway.

—

"That, I did…" Deepak was sitting on a chair in a dimly lit room, facing Sub Inspector Afzal Hussain. His face was badly bruised and hands cuffed to the table. "Why?" Afzal asked.

"Guess, I wanted to do something for my sister, for once." Embarrassed and ashamed, Deepak rested his head on the table.

"So you did that. You think she wanted that?" Afzal lit a cigarette and blew smoke in Deepak's face."

"After that?" Afzal turned to his watch and yawned, "Are chandu, ek chai laiye chhote ke liye…" Afzal stepped out for a break, leaving Deepak alone with his thoughts. And it was certain that a man with nothing but his thoughts is bound to recall the worst of his memories.

Deepak was defining and reciting his actions as if he were getting some clarity from it, searching for redemption, or some sense of understanding—or discomfort—toward his actions. But all he could feel was the unease that he couldn't get rid of. Maybe it's because he hadn't taken a bath in a week, having been punished, beaten into submission, and forced to confess. It felt like a time travel journey to the moment he shot something—someone—with limbs, with a life.

"When was this?" Afzal was munching on chips, some soft cakes on the table, while Deepak entirely disgusted by any food, stared blankly at the darkest corner of the room.

"Just before you arrested me, I guess." Sleep-deprived, and barely holding his back against anything. "So, you never actually got the chance to kill before that." Afzal could sense the lack of primal disgust of a dead body amongst civilians, with normal people, it's something unbearable but either the increased involvement in crime prone areas or the inherent drive was the reason for Deepak to slip this deep into the rabbit hole of crime.

"Nobody gets to touch my family," Deepak's confessions weren't something he was proud of, so there's nothing to boast about but to provide clarity of how circumstances and poor judgment of self's character could lead you to situations you can't escape.

"We'll see about that." With a smirk on his face, Afzal took another drag. "So, you're saying you're innocent of his murder."

"I never said that. It was a burst of anger. I made a mistake."

"That's more than a couple, I think." Afzal turned to the file and started looking through the documents. "Impressive resume, huh."

"I will plead guilty, so get me whatever imprisonment you all think would be better. I don't have anything else to say."

Afzal stood up and walked around, "You're too popular to arrest without crackers. So, why the gangs? You were confident and wealthy enough to start your own business."

This is where it struck him. Deepak could've stepped back, disappeared, and lived without any criminal record if not for that one day. Nobody really knew him personally,

"This has nothing to do with you." But Deepak realized what drove him to that range of emotions. Afzal burst into laughter, then suddenly slapped Deepak, slamming his head onto the table.

"Do I look like I'm writing a biography? Now, be good. And when I ask a question, you tell me. You tell me everything." Afzal sat back down, Deepak's head still on the table,

"I tried my best. Amazing scores, academics, practicals. He liked music too, so I learned that too… but he never had time." Deepak stayed down, not bothering to look at Afzal, as if he were habitual to the beatings and slamming. He'd find his share of comfort however he could, within these pretty much permanent circumstances, while the cops and people of law, like Afzal sipped cold drinks.

"Fuck, you have a boyfriend?" slightly displeased and disgusted, Afzal put the drink aside.

"Baapu" Deepak turned to Afzal, for once, a bit annoyed by the occasional sense of humor.

"Didi had a lot going on with training, practice, matches, state and nationals. Maa was ignored and suppressed more often, so she barely talked about things like these. And baapu was always busy with taps, canals, people, politics, money, and everybody else's personal affairs."

And these criminals were once accepted and praised for being daring and bold. "And after a while, you were there…" Afzal stood up and left, while Deepak folded his hands and laid his head on them, going for a nap.

—

The thudding sound of the door slamming still echoed in her mind. The loud banging on the door sent a ripple of tension through the house, and Gehna and Deepak both knew exactly who the police were there for.

"Kheda ke Sardaar, hamara pyaar bula raha hai, bahar aaiye! Kangan laaye hain thare vaaste!" Afzal Hussain's mocking voice rang out, his words laced with a cruel mix of sarcasm and authority. Afzal was just another corrupt cop, always chasing money and opportunities to rise through the ranks. But today, he wasn't after money—he was here for a much bigger prize: Gehna's brother.

Sheela, startled and confused, opened the door cautiously. "Who's this? Why are you shouting?" she asked, only to be pushed aside as the police officers—men and women—stormed into the house, their presence overwhelming and aggressive.

"Gehna! There are policemen here, what have you done?" Her mother's voice echoed from the ground floor, panic-stricken. The cops began searching the house, and Gehna stood on the rooftop with Deepak, watching them surround their home. She realized this was the end for her brother. There was no escaping it now.

This wasn't the moment for apologies, nor for promises of change. No matter how much Deepak had wanted to turn over a new leaf, the weight of his past misdeeds was something he couldn't outrun. The consequences had finally caught up with him, and Gehna knew it. Still, desperate for some mercy, she tried talking to the female cops and, in a last-ditch effort, called her father, Nandlal.

"Baapu, they're here to take him," Gehna's voice trembled as she handed the phone to Afzal, her hands shaking. Afzal took the phone, but as he turned to Gehna, he was momentarily stunned. His gaze lingered on her, tracing the sweat that beaded along her neckline, his eyes dark with desire. For a moment, his purpose seemed to slip away, overtaken by something more primal.

"Bahar nikal, saale!" a cop shouted from outside, but Afzal didn't react. He was lost, captivated by Gehna's desperate eyes. He could sense her vulnerability, and a twisted idea began to form in his mind. He wanted her—more than just a fleeting moment of power, he wanted to own her.

"Re, sab neeche aao, koi haath mat lagao bhai ko!" Afzal called out to the others, his tone shifting as he gently attempted to touch Gehna, a sly grin spreading across his face. She stepped back instinctively, and Afzal, undeterred, folded his hands as if in mock respect. "Sorry ji, I didn't know he was your brother. Vaise, naam kya hai aapka?" His smile was venomous.

Gehna, though shaken, recognized what was happening. She understood that in that moment, Afzal's lust had become his weakness. If a man wanted a woman, she had power over him. How far that power could go, she wasn't sure—but she needed to find out.

"I don't want my brother to go to jail," she said firmly, her voice steady even as she wiped the sweat from her face and chest. Afzal turned around, considering her words. For him, the brother was just an obstacle. He could let Deepak go if it meant having Gehna in his grasp.

"Okay ji, done samjho aap," Afzal agreed, a wicked smile lighting up his face. He felt as though he had found his way into her heart—or at least, he thought he had.

As Afzal sat there, smugly munching on chips and sipping tea in the veranda, the other officers stood outside, guarding the perimeter. Gehna sat quietly beside Deepak, her mind racing. Sheela watched from across the room, her eyes filled with a mixture of worry and disgust. Afzal's attention, however, never strayed far from Gehna, even as her father, Nandlal, arrived.

Nandlal, visibly furious, stormed into the house, his eyes scanning the scene. The police vans parked outside, the house surrounded—it was enough to make any father's blood boil. Afzal, seeing him approach, quickly stood up, trying to smooth things over.

"Arrey, papaji! If I had known he was your son, I would've straightened him out and sent him home myself. He's like my brother!" Afzal spoke with an exaggerated familiarity, desperate to gain Nandlal's favor. But all the while, his eyes kept darting back to Gehna, who had discreetly pulled her dupatta over her chest, hiding herself from his predatory gaze now that her father was present.

Afzal thought he had played his cards right, but Gehna knew this game was far from over.

Nandlal's rage was palpable. "Do I look like your father? Or did I sleep with your mother? Don't you dare call me that." His voice boomed through the house. He had dealt with political rivals and underhanded tactics before, but the gravity of this situation—the police vans, the officers everywhere—left him baffled. Why was Deepak involved in this? What had his son gotten himself into? The air was thick with tension, and Nandlal wanted every cop out of his house immediately.

"Sir," Afzal's voice was low but firm, cutting through the room like a knife, "This isn't some petty crime. We're not talking about pickpocketing or smoking weed. Your son, Deepak, is involved in a turf war, drug trafficking, and just yesterday, he killed five people."

Nandlal and Sheela stood frozen, their faces drained of color. Gehna, however, was the most shaken. She turned her face away from Deepak, horrified, as though she'd expected some reckless behavior from her brother but never imagined something so dark and violent.

"Mera beta kahin nahi jaega," Nandlal barked, still refusing to accept the weight of the situation. His voice was filled with the same denial that had carried him through years of ignoring his responsibilities.

Afzal's lips curled into a mocking smile. "Toh beti le jaaun?" His tone was casual, but the audacity of his words hit Gehna like a slap. He was offering a life-for-life exchange, using her as a bargaining chip, and Nandlal didn't even flinch. Gehna looked at her father, searching his face for any sign of protection, but all she found was helplessness.

"Daffa ho ja!" Nandlal tried to assert his authority, shouting in desperation, but it was futile. Afzal wasn't listening. "I didn't bring the police here just for show," he said dryly, pulling on his cap and signaling his men to move in. Deepak was handcuffed within seconds. Afzal turned to Gehna briefly, a flicker of disappointment in his eyes before he looked away.

"Baapu…sorry. Baapu!" Deepak's cries echoed through the house as the police dragged him out. Nandlal remained frozen, unable to move or speak, the weight of his guilt and failures crushing him. He slumped to the floor, and Gehna rushed to catch him, holding herself together even as she felt her world falling apart.

Meanwhile, Afzal, sitting in his jeep with a strange look of dissatisfaction on his face, drove off.

Chapter - 3

LET'S START

Back in her jeep, Gehna was lost in thought, combing through a notepad filled with scattered information—names, events, random pieces of data that were beginning to fit together like the edges of a puzzle. She squinted slightly, reading over the notes as her jeep rattled down the dusty village road, the faint hum of voices and village life fading into the background. Just then, her phone rang on the passenger seat, its unfamiliar number catching her attention. Her eyes narrowing slightly as she reached over to answer it.

"Sarpanch sahiba, kaisi hain aap?" The voice on the other end held an oddly familiar ring, something she'd heard before, but she struggled to place it—years blurred the memory.

"Kaun?" she replied cautiously.

"Afzal hu..." the voice continued, barely finishing his name when Gehna's foot stomped on the brake, sending the jeep skidding to the side, halting just a hair's breadth from the canal. She gripped the wheel, knuckling white, her breath quickening as a surge of memories flooded back.

"The one who thrashed your brother in jail..." Gehna took her time getting some kind of hint to understand who this person is but immediately when he mentioned the incident, everything flooded back in ehr mind.

"Tu, Mujhse kyun call kiya hai? Rakh phone." Gehna immediately hung up.

But he called again, the words came out like an accusation, loaded with everything she suddenly remembered about him and the fallout that had turned her family's life upside down.

"So you do remember me." Afzal's tone sounded almost pleased, casual, as if expecting her reaction.

Gehna's face hardened, her response sharp and wary. "Hmmm… Bolo," she muttered, her intuition already piecing together why he might be calling.

"I just heard you're the sarpanch of your district now. Looks like your father stepped aside," he said with a smug familiarity that dug under her skin, each word laced with the same arrogant tone she'd known him for.

"It's been years," Gehna shot back, her voice tightening. "Why now? And who even gave you my number?"

Afzal chuckled softly. "Didn't need to; it's public info. Your village falls under my jurisdiction. I'm the new Superintendent here. Just calling to give you a heads-up. I know there were… tensions after I left with your brother, but I was just doing my job."

"There's no need to bring that up." She felt the burn of anger behind her words, holding back the deeper hurt she never allowed herself to express, especially about her brother.

"Of course, as you wish," he continued smoothly. "So, how about a meet-up? It's been a long time."

The suggestion left a bitter taste. She could sense his motives, even over the phone. Having him near, now when she was planning to secure her brother's release, was dangerous—his position could make him a threat if he grew suspicious.

"We'll see." She ended the call, tossing the phone onto the passenger seat. She gripped the steering wheel, letting out a slow breath to ground herself. He was a problem she didn't need, and she wasn't an assassin skilled enough to eliminate him without risking detection—he was too well-connected, too experienced in handling criminals to let her slip under his radar.

—

"Are you okay?" Mother gently stroked Gehna's hair as they sat together in silence.

"Not right now, but we'll all be fine. I'll take care of everything." They remained quiet, the unspoken weight of their shared burdens hanging between them.

"Arrey, Deepak!" Nandlal's voice rang out from elsewhere in the house, his footsteps heavy as he searched for something. Sheela and Gehna, hearing Deepak's name, rushed out of the room only to find Nandlal wandering about, phone in hand, speaking excitedly to someone on a video call.

"Deepak ka phone hai!" Nandlal exclaimed, his face lit up with joy. He sat down on the ground, eyes fixed on the screen, as Sheela descended the stairs to join in on the conversation. Gehna, however, lingered on the steps, watching her parents share this rare moment of happiness with their son.

"How are you calling on this phone? A video call? Do they allow this?" Nandlal, grinning ear to ear, barely knew what to say, too happy just to see Deepak's face.

"Yes, I get 25 minutes a week to talk to everyone," Deepak explained. On the other side of the screen, he held a laptop, assisted by a policeman. He had been waiting for this moment, to see his family, for what felt like ages.

"How are you? How are you eating?" Sheela, even the mother, couldn't help but focus on his well-being. "I'll send something good with Gehna, don't share it with anyone." It stung Gehna—he wasn't away on a business trip; he was in jail. But that truth, they all knew, couldn't be voiced. Not now.

For a moment, the room felt light, everyone content just to be together in this fleeting moment.

"So, what's going on? Where's Didi?" Deepak asked, his face lighting up when he noticed Gehna smiling down from the stairs.

"What are you doing up there? Come down," Nandlal called, his joy evident as he wanted the family to be complete again. But Gehna, watching her parents laugh and talk, knew what was missing. It was him.

"So, when are you coming back?" Sheela asked, immediately regretting the question. She glanced away, as if trying to avoid the harsh reality, while Nandlal forced a smile, coughing awkwardly to mask his discomfort. "Beta, tu aaja ghar. Jaise ho, jab ho. Bas phone karte rehna. Badi yaad aati hai teri." Nandlal's voice cracked as tears welled in his eyes. He handed the phone to Gehna, who sat at her parents' feet, both of them now seated on the couch.

"Kya jail tod ke aaya toh achha nahi lagega," Deepak joked, his voice faltering as emotion crept in. He tried to hold back tears, not wanting to break in front of his family, then turned to his sister. "Re, Didi, tujhe ek chitthi aayi hogi, zara dekhiyo." Gehna glanced toward the gate and found an envelope from the jail, hidden among the pile of mail.

"Maa, Baapu, yeh hai meri kamaai. 4-5 saalon se thoda kaam-dhanda dekh liya hai yahan," Deepak continued as Gehna handed the envelope to Sheela. She opened it and found money inside.

"Maa ko ek badhiya saaree dilana aur Bapu ke liye ek badhiya kurta. Yeh tere pe chhoda! Itna sambhal rakha hai, thoda aur dekh le." Deepak's voice broke, and he turned away from the camera, unable to hold back his tears any longer.

Gehna's hands trembled as she held the phone. Deepak wasn't a criminal anymore. He was just a boy trying to make something of his life, even in the bleakest of circumstances.

"Aur meri mithai ka kya?" Gehna asked, her voice trembling, rough with emotion. Behind her, Sheela hid her face in her saree, trying to stifle her sobs.

"Jo aa jaaye, dekh liyo. Main aur bhej dunga, pakka, agle mahine," Deepak replied, his eyes scanning the faces of his family, taking in how much he had been missed—even after all these years. But something still felt off.

"Baapu, tu yeh bata. Daaru chhodega ya nahi? Didi bata rahi thi mujhe... Kahan kahan leke doge tujhe is umar mein? Kya chahta hai? Ib clean kar de," Deepak suddenly turned to his father. Nandlal looked frail, too weak to bear the burden of his son's words, his cough interrupting his sentences. Deepak could hear the slur in his voice, could see the toll alcohol had taken.

"Tu aajaega toh sab chhod dunga," Nandlal replied quietly, wiping away his tears.

"Mere aane tak toh tik jaa," Deepak's voice cracked under the weight of his plea. "Mujhe. Mujhe yahan se... tujhe fookne nahi nikalna hai. Samajh le." These were the hardest words Deepak had ever said, words he had never wanted to say, but he had no choice. He fought to maintain his composure, but the dam broke, and he wept openly. His family wept with him.

Neither Gehna nor Sheela could hold back their tears. They had been trying so hard to stay strong, to be brave for each other, but the weight of it all—the unspoken fears, the hope, the pain—had finally become too much.

Reaching her house, she stepped out to unlock the main gate, catching sight of police vans and jeeps parked on her street. She paused, her gaze following the officers and the vehicles.

“But… what if I could use them,” she murmured, the hint of a plan forming.

Climbing back into her jeep, Gehna grabbed her phone, saved Afzal's contact, and dialed.

"Khana milein," she said, not waiting for pleasantries.

"Chhavni Mata Mandir ke piche vale bargad par," he replied, a note of satisfaction slipping into his voice, as if he'd been expecting her call.

"Time?"

"Shaam 6 baje."

Gehna hung up, her lips curving in a faint smile. But the moment she let go of the phone, her expression turned razor-sharp. The glimmer of amusement vanished, replaced by an intense focus. If she played this right, she could turn every piece of Afzal's network to her advantage.

Under the towering banyan tree in the heart of the village, a group of elders sat on khats, puffing on hookahs. The village was slowly gathering, people walking or running toward the Panchayat stage, where makeshift mats and cushions were spread out, worn with age and use. Some bamboo chairs stood beside the khats for the younger members of the council.

"Arrey, gram pradhan aa gayi bhaiya! Utho utho!" The buzz went through the crowd as Gehna's jeep pulled up. Everyone stood as she stepped out, accompanied by a few women from the village.

"Hanji! Shall we begin?" Gehna asked, taking her place in the center, surrounded by the elders, her gaze steady as she faced the villagers.

A villager named Dhannu stood up, folding his hands in respect. His wife stood beside him, noticeably taller than him, a quiet yet stark contrast.

"Ma'am saheb, I'm Dhannu, and this... this is my wife santoshi." Dhannu's voice cracked as he introduced himself, a mix of sorrow and frustration echoing in his words.

"Mahraaj! I've been scammed! I want my money back. I married this woman, and I was told she's fair and healthy." Dhannu, a well-built man, folded his hands, clearly upset. His wife, standing beside him, tried to pull her drape tighter, covering her face and upper body as much as she could.

"She works the fields, fixes the fan, and can do more pushups than I can! I'm sure she's a man," Dhannu complained, his frustration obvious.

Gehna, trying to make sense of the situation, raised an eyebrow. "Shaadi se pehle, mandir-wandir nahi ghumaya kya isne?" she asked, wondering if Dhannu hadn't noticed something earlier.

"Ji, bas barf ka gola khilaya tha," Dhannu replied in a lowered, quiet, manly, defeated tone. Some men standing in the crowd chuckled quietly.

"Kya kar diya, bhai, deeware lagai ghodi. Dekho do mardon ki jodi!" someone from the crowd shouted, and everyone burst into laughter.

"Shaanti!" Gehna shouted, silencing the crowd immediately.

"Zara pallu uthaiye," Gehna said, asking the wife to reveal her face. The woman hesitated at first but then did as asked. She was a strikingly beautiful woman, her strong build only adding to her unique presence.

"Kya malook chhori hai!" someone in the crowd exclaimed.

"Ghana chauka sauda hai, bhai! Kya kartab karegi," another man commented, but before he could finish, Gehna stormed over and slapped him hard across the face.

"Teri behen bhi naachegi kya bistar pe? Tameez bachi hai ya sab gayi?" Gehna fumed, her anger cutting through the air. The man was quickly pulled away by others, and the crowd fell silent.

Gehna returned to her seat, calming herself with a cough before continuing. "Listen, share the responsibilities. Work together. There's nothing wrong here from what I can see. Grow up." Her words left Dhannu speechless, and the matter was settled.

As the sun dipped toward the horizon and the panchayat meeting was nearing its end, Gehna stood up once more. She had something important to say, something that had been on her mind for a while.

"We're the elders of this village, and we need to make better judgment. There's a lot we missed by not going to school," she began, her voice steady, "but there's also so much we've learned from life that school couldn't teach us. It's all about choices—both are important, but we need a balance of both. So never hesitate to send your children to school. The future is unpredictable."

The villagers clapped in agreement, their faces showing they understood the value of her words. Gehna's message had struck a chord, and the day's meeting ended on a note of reflection and growth.

"Now," Gehna said, standing up to address the gathering, "I have something I want to discuss with all of you." She paused, scanning the crowd. "Can anyone tell me who's the smartest person in the world?"

The question seemed simple enough, and everyone perked up, excited to participate. Gehna's leadership had always encouraged open conversation, and no one ever felt afraid to share their thoughts. The air was filled with a sense of anticipation.

"Hassan…Hassanburg!" a young man in his twenties called out, standing eagerly.

"Hassanburg?" Gehna's interest was piqued, curious to hear more about this person she wasn't familiar with.

"Pradhan ji, I saw him in a show! A foreign series. He's a genius!"

"It's not a movie, it's a TV series," another young man chimed in, trying to correct his peer. It was clear that the conversation had veered into their knowledge of foreign cinema and shows, not the actual question at hand.

"So, you're telling me he's a character from TV?" Gehna's tone shifted slightly, her excitement waning. "Beta, he's an actor, just pretending to be smart. That's acting, not real life." She motioned for the two young men to sit down, which they did, clearly a bit embarrassed.

"Anyone else?" Gehna prompted, looking for a more meaningful response.

"Parth Gokesh! Vishwa Parth Gokesh!" another young man stood up confidently, his polished appearance signaling he might have some formal education.

"Who's Gokesh Rajoo?" Gehna asked, interested but not wanting to make him uncomfortable by questioning his knowledge too much.

"He was the number one ranked player in the world for 21 months. It's the sixth-longest time anyone's held that position. Oh, and he's Indian," he added proudly.

Gehna nodded, satisfied. This was the kind of answer she had hoped for, someone real and accomplished. As the discussion continued, this young man listed off other notable names—Hussain Baloch, the fastest marathon runner, Sunil Kumble, India's cricket legend known for his accuracy, and Amandeep Singh, the famous hockey player.

Realizing the value of such talent, Gehna decided on the spot to create an opportunity for the village youth. She announced a competition that would grant scholarships for higher education, something that left the villagers impressed. The idea of giving their children a chance to study and pursue greatness resonated deeply, and the meeting ended on a hopeful note.

Suddenly, Gehna's phone rang. She glanced at the caller ID and immediately her expression darkened. The shift in her mood was palpable, but she maintained her composure as she politely excused herself from the gathering.

Driving away, her thoughts drifted back to the argument she'd had with her brother Deepak on the terrace of their home.

——-

A white ambassador car, its red police light flashing, cut smoothly through traffic. Motorists grumbled, annoyed by the usual sight of government vehicles using their authority to bypass everyone. But inside, Afzal barely noticed. He was lost in his phone, playing a game until a call from Gehna interrupted him. A smile spread across his face as he answered.

"You there?" he asked casually, reclining further into the back seat. He found his deodorant, and sprayed it liberally—even inside his pants, grinning at his reflection in the rearview mirror.

He pulled up in front, stepped out, looking every bit the confident, commanding officer. He walked toward the back.

Gehna sat on a wooden bed, sitting there against the open fields for anyone to rest, watching Afzal approach. She had been thinking about how to deal with a man who held so much power over the police—and, by extension, over her and her family. But as Afzal walked toward her, she realized that this wasn't the same man she had met before. He wasn't the casual, somewhat charming officer who had dropped by her house to chat after arresting her brother.

This was a man who had once pursued her relentlessly, promising he'd return but disappearing from her life for years. Now, he was back, but Gehna wasn't sure whether this was a new beginning or just the continuation of a dangerous game.

But facing him, Gehna realized he was still the same idiot. The gaze he directed at her scanned her from top to bottom, lingering on her chest and bosom. She knew navigating this would be tricky, but not impossible.

"How are you, Gehna?" They shook hands as he sat beside her. "I knew we'd find each other someday. To be honest, I was going to come over to your house a few weeks ago since I've been promoted to SP. Now, there's no reason we can't be together." Afzal didn't realize that he had just confirmed the affection and attention she needed from him for her plan to succeed. There was no need to plot or reveal too much; everything could unfold at its own pace.

"Well, the circumstances under which we met weren't ideal. I couldn't have any affection toward you while you were handcuffing my brother," Gehna said, pausing for effect. She could see the interest and desperation flickering in his eyes. "But..."

"But...?" he prompted, leaning closer. Afzal's smile broadened, and she could see his ego swell with her praise.

"So, what have you been up to? It's been eight years," she asked, keen to perform a background check and understand if there was anything she should be cautious about.

"If you're asking if I'm married or not, then yes..." He looked away, fiddling with a newspaper, trying to fold it into some semblance of a paper boat.

"Nice," Gehna said, chuckling. "Any girlfriends?" As she picked up another piece of tissue, she tried her hand at folding it into something that made even less sense than his creation.

They both glanced at their failed attempts and burst into laughter.

"You're really bad at this," she teased, eyeing his creation. "That looks like a drop of shit."

Afzal, taken aback, stammered, "Done by a pony," trying to deflect her comment, but Gehna just looked at him with a confused expression.

"So, what's up with your Pradhan ji? How's pitaji?" Afzal switched the subject, calling her father "pitaji" to show his interest in her, which felt oddly forward for someone she hadn't seen in years. The obsession he had—or still had—was unsettling to a certain extent, as it seemed to have no boundaries.

"There's a new pradhan now," Gehna replied, carefully choosing her words. "The old one became drunk and started smoking heavily, to the point where he's now on bed rest." She deliberately avoided mentioning her brother Deepak, hoping to keep Afzal clueless about the deeper issues in her family.

"I'm the new pradhan," Gehna declared before he could steer the conversation elsewhere, trying to establish equal standing between them. She wanted him to see that she wasn't trying to take advantage of him, nor was he being scammed.

"Congratulations!" he said, leaning in for a hug. She complied, returning the embrace. "I've always wanted to see what it feels like to be in authority, to have people under your command. It's fun." Gehna knew about Afzal's superiority complex—how much he relished giving orders and being in charge. She needed to provide him with common ground.

"Nice!" Afzal said, admiring her new attitude and the similarities in their perspectives toward the people they governed.

"I just wanted something fulfilling," Gehna continued, keeping her tone earnest. "I mean, even you wouldn't want to marry someone who's just a cook and cleans the house all day." She watched his expression closely, gauging his reaction.

"Of course not," he replied, nodding enthusiastically. "You need someone with ambition, someone who can contribute to your success, just like you're doing now. We're cut from the same cloth, Gehna."

"Exactly," she said, leaning in slightly, reinforcing the bond they were starting to form. "We have the potential to create something greater, don't you think?"

Afzal's eyes sparkled with ambition. "Absolutely. We could work together to make the village a better place. You have the power, and I have the authority. Imagine the changes we could bring!"

Gehna felt a flicker of excitement. This was the foothold she needed. "I'd like that," she replied, matching his enthusiasm. "We could do great things."

"Then it's settled," he declared, his voice brimming with confidence. "We'll team up, and I'll make sure you have all the support you need from the police."

Gehna nodded, feeling a surge of determination. She had to stay sharp and keep her wits about her, but she was now standing at the precipice of a partnership that could change everything. However, she knew she had to tread carefully, balancing the line between using Afzal's ambition for her benefit while ensuring that she never became just another pawn in his game.

He held her hands and kissed them softly. "Don't worry, we can be together now. I have everything we need. I've earned everything for you. Let's make peace with the past and find a future together." Afzal was trying to get too comfortable, too soon.

"I don't think now is the right time," Gehna replied reluctantly, pulling her hands out of his grasp. "You know I'm Hindu, and you're Muslim. I don't care about that, but my father is gravely ill right now, and I can't put this on him." Afzal nodded, but the desperation in his eyes was still fresh. Every move he made was calculated, and he was the most crucial part of the plan Gehna had in mind.

"The thing is, I need your help," Gehna continued, launching into her carefully crafted dialogue. "This is something I can't shake off." She was laying the groundwork for a specific set of responses, leading toward that all-important "Yes, I'll do it" that she needed from him—an unconditional agreement to whatever she had planned.

"What's going on? Tell me," Afzal said, his curiosity piqued, eager to understand what held so much power over their bond.

"Actually, let's just leave it. I don't want to get you into any trouble with all this SP stuff. I think I should leave now," Gehna said, trying to stand up. But Afzal held her hand, and she slid it away, asking him to step aside. She knew she had to handle him with care and maintain her ground; she couldn't afford to slip and give him the upper hand.

Just as she was about to leave the table, he said, "You should trust someone to build trust. Never look back if I say no. I just need a chance." Afzal stood up, knowing she would never come back if she left this time.

Gehna stood still without looking back, preparing for her final move. She steadily walked toward the gate. "Come on, yaar! You can't just say all these things and leave like nothing happened…"

"I…" She paused, turning back to gauge Afzal's reaction. He seemed curious, eager to follow wherever this conversation led. Stepping closer, she leaned into his ear, her voice barely above a whisper. "I want to kidnap someone."

She stood there, close enough for him to catch a whiff of the expensive perfume she had bought. The scent enveloped him, and he was already enchanted, wanting to be closer.

"That's all?" he asked, looking up at her, a smirk spreading across his face. Gehna sensed that if it came to a challenge against his huge ego, he would rise to it—and he did just as she had planned. He immediately pulled out his phone, took out the SIM card, and broke it in half. Confused, Gehna stood there, unsure of what to think.

"Can I have your phone?" Afzal asked. Gehna handed hers over, still puzzled. He took out her SIM card as well, stood up, and went to the kitchen, tossing both into the blender and crushing them.

"If you're serious about this kidnapping of yours, we can't be seen together from now on. We need new cell phones," he explained. Gehna was still trying to process the situation. "This guy is dangerous; he knows this world..." she thought to herself, a mix of admiration and concern swirling in her mind.

Feeling a rush of determination, Gehna pulled him closer and kissed him. This was the commitment needed to seal their fate; both Gehna and Afzal were now bound together in their criminal endeavor. He stepped out and rummaged through his car, returning with two new cell phones. He handed her one with a fresh SIM card.

"Now we're off the grid," he said, his eyes sparkling with excitement and mischief. "But remember, this is just the beginning."

Gehna nodded, feeling the weight of their decision settle around them. She couldn't shake the sense of danger, but the thrill of the unknown was intoxicating. Together, they were ready to step into a world that could change everything, holding the power of their fate in their own hands.

"Text me once you reach home," Afzal said, a smile on his face as if he had achieved something monumental. He was about to leave the café, feeling like a knight in shining armor ready to save his princess.

"Wait!" Gehna shouted, halting him in his tracks. "I don't know how to use this phone."

Afzal's smile faltered as the realization hit him: she was illiterate. It contradicted everything he had hoped for and planned. Now, they were going to sit together as he taught her how to navigate the device. Yet, amidst the unexpected turn, there was a sense of relief; he could spend more time with her.

"Alright, let's get started," he said, trying to mask his disappointment with enthusiasm. He stepped outside, instructing his driver to send the others home, leaving the car for just the two of them.

"First, let's turn it on." He pressed the power button and handed the phone back to her, watching intently as her eyes widened in fascination. "You'll see the home screen now."

Gehna touched the screen cautiously, a mixture of curiosity and apprehension in her demeanor. "What do I do now?" she asked, glancing at him for guidance.

"See those icons? Those are apps. You can open them by tapping on them. Here, let's start with this one," he said, pointing to the messaging app.

"Messaging?" she echoed, intrigued.

"Yeah, it's how you'll text me. Just tap on it." Afzal's heart raced as he watched her explore the device. This was a small step into a world that had been beyond her reach until now.

Gehna tapped the app, and the screen opened up, revealing a blank message. "Now what?" she asked, looking at him expectantly.

"Wait," Afzal switched the normal keyboard to hindi keyboard, "Now, tell me something you'd like to text me." Afzal held the phone for both of them to see, getting closer to her, touching shoulder. "I'll teach you how to type on a hindi keyboard."

Gehna kept her eyes locked on the phone, curling her hair behind her ears, letting afzal see her *jhumka*.

"Kaise ho, afzal?"

Afzal heard that and pointed to the keyboard with a smile on his face. He was amused and enjoying this moment.

"Yeh saare shabd hain, aur maatra lagaane ke liye yeh vaali line hai," he typed and showed her how to build a sentence.

"Now, you can type my name and another message," he instructed. "Or, you can simply tap on my contact if you have saved it."

"Okay, I can do that," she said, her confidence slowly building. Afzal couldn't help but feel a surge of pride at her determination.

As she focused on the screen, he took a moment to admire her—her concentration, the way her brows furrowed slightly as she tried to understand. It was endearing, and he felt a sense of connection growing between them.

"Got it!" Gehna exclaimed suddenly, her face lighting up with accomplishment. "Now I just hit send, right?"

"Exactly!" Afzal encouraged, leaning in closer. "Just like that."

With a triumphant smile, she pressed the button, sending the message. "I did it!"

"Great job!" Afzal cheered, feeling a warmth spread through him. "You're a quick learner."

Gehna laughed, a sound that seemed to brighten the small space around them. "I never thought I'd be texting anyone."

"Well, now you can text me anytime," he replied, his voice softer. "We're in this together."

Gehna absorbed everything Afzal taught her, from searching on Google to tracking locations and navigating maps. He patiently guided her through each step, ensuring she understood the intricacies of the smartphone. He encouraged her to explore, showing her how to find information quickly and efficiently.

"Look, if you want to find a place, just type the name here," Afzal explained, pointing to the search bar. "And the map will show you the way."

Gehna's eyes sparkled with newfound knowledge. "This is amazing!" she exclaimed, tapping the screen as she searched for nearby cafes and shops. Each successful search boosted her confidence, and she was eager to learn more.

"Just remember, the more you play around with it, the more comfortable you'll become," he advised. "Curiosity is key."

Gehna nodded, her determination palpable. She was not merely learning for the sake of it; she had a commitment to a much larger plan—one that would secure a better future for herself and her family. There was a fire in her eyes that made it clear she was willing to do anything to achieve her goals.

"Can you help me with something else?" she asked, her tone shifting from light-hearted to serious.

"Of course," Afzal replied, intrigued.

"How can I find people, like their location, or phone? Suppose my father went somewhere and I have to reach him." Gehna added an example to justify her motives.

"Alright. We can set up some alerts for when he uses his phone, and I'll teach you how to access his location using apps. But you have to be careful. "

"I understand," she replied, determination lacing her words.

As Afzal guided her through the process of installing tracking apps and setting up alerts, he couldn't help but admire her tenacity. Gehna wasn't just a victim of her circumstances; she was a warrior, fighting for her family in a world that had given them so little.

"Once you've got this down, you'll be able to keep an eye on him," he said, ensuring she grasped each step. "And if anything happens, you'll know right away."

"Okay," Gehna said, her voice softening.

"I'll always have your back," he promised, feeling a bond forming between them that went beyond the immediate situation. It was a partnership forged in the fires of adversity, one where both were willing to risk everything for the sake of the other.

As they continued their lesson, the air thick with unspoken understanding and shared ambition, Gehna felt a renewed sense of purpose. She wasn't just learning how to navigate a phone; she was equipping herself for the battles ahead, ready to fight for the future she envisioned.

Chapter - 4

GRANDMASTER

Nandlal came to the table, downing the last bit of whiskey from his glass before setting it down on the dinner table. He glanced around, finding no one. But as soon as the pressure cooker whistled, he realized Sheela was in the kitchen, preparing something for lunch. It had been a while since he last saw his daughter, Gehna, and though he tried not to show it, the thought bothered him. Despite everything, he worried about her. Moments later, Sheela appeared, carrying a few boiled potatoes and a bowl of cold water. She sat beside him on the veranda, quietly peeling the potatoes, dipping her hand into the water when they became too hot.

“Where's she?” Nandlal asked, knowing full well that Sheela would have an answer. As detached as he had become, he knew she always kept track of everyone in the house, asking where they were headed, no matter who it was.

"Upstairs, in her room," Sheela replied, not looking up, her voice edged with frustration. Clearly, she was too annoyed to even engage in a conversation about it.

"It's been a while, I haven't seen her," Nandlal said, leaning back in his chair, his speech slightly slurred from the alcohol.

“It's better this way,” Sheela finally said, peeling another potato. “She wouldn't want to see you drunk at noon.”

“It's afternoon,” Nandlal muttered defensively.

“And that's a reason for you to drink.”

Sheela glanced up, her irritation clear as she looked at him briefly before returning to her task. She set the perfectly peeled potato aside and rested her hand in the bowl of cold water for a moment.

Rising from her seat, Sheela took the plate of potatoes and the bowl with her as she walked back to the kitchen. "I'm making aloo pyaaz ka paratha. Let me know if you want some snacks. Not that you'll eat lunch anyway." Hearing her words, Nandlal poured himself a glass of water, gulping it down, then sat there staring at the empty glass, lost in thought.

Upstairs, Gehna had locked herself in her room, consumed by her research. Her sole focus was gathering every detail about Vishwa Parth Gokesh, a grandmaster for the past decade, winner of numerous tournaments, and ranked fifth globally. She set her phone down and turned to her diary, where she meticulously documented every piece of information she might need.

"So, what do we know about this Parth?" she muttered to herself, having spent enough time alone to start talking aloud. "Five-time world champion, the best I can find. A simple guy with little to no security. Scheduled to visit Delhi for an event between Feb 25 and Feb 28..." She crossed off the necessary details and reached for her phone again, trying to find information about his accommodations, but nothing came up in the news.

An idea struck her. She turned to social media, remembering the advice from S.P. Afzal:

"Everybody's starving for attention—whether it's how they dress, how they appear, talk, walk, or live. They're bound to post it all on social media. Out of sight is out of mind for people, and these types live for attention." Afzal understood not just criminals, but human behavior. He had proven useful for the plan, though Gehna knew he needed to be kept in check. No man was immune to the temptation of getting what he wanted.

"Anyways..." Gehna whispered as she scrolled through social media. Soon enough, she found Parth's profile, noticing that he had been active just two hours ago. That meant he was likely to post the details she needed.

“Gehna! Open the gate!” Her mother’s sudden pounding on the door startled her. Gehna jumped out of bed, quickly switching on the lights. Looking around at the tidy room, she braced herself for Sheela’s scolding—it was unlike her to stay locked up like this for days. Hesitantly, she unlocked the door.

Sheela walked in, scanning the room before sitting on Gehna’s bed, visibly trying to calm herself. "What’s going on with you? It’s been three days. You don’t come down for dinner, you don’t go to the panchayat office anymore, you don’t talk to anyone. I’m constantly making excuses for you. It’s not just you and your father who live here, I’m alive too.” Sheela’s voice cracked as she fidgeted with the drape of her saree, fighting back tears.

Gehna suddenly realized the flaw in her plan—she had been so focused on executing it that she hadn’t accounted for the strain it would put on her family. She couldn’t afford for her home to fall apart while she worked to save it.

“I’m just a little tired,” Gehna said softly, lying down with her head on Sheela’s lap. Sheela began to gently brush her hair, the tension easing slightly.

—

"Adha kat gaya hai, thoda aur kat le. Watch TV, news, serials. But stop drinking and smoking. It’s enough." Deepak’s voice held a note of pleading, though he knew his words alone wouldn’t change anything. All he could do was say what he could, but he had no illusions about their power.

The call abruptly disconnected—it had been exactly 23 minutes. Gehna expected her brother to argue with the policeman for cutting it short, but this much time, this brief connection, was enough to bring her family together. Just these few minutes of communication were enough to keep their bond strong, to give them a bit of motivation, a little more strength to hold on.

It wasn't just for Deepak, sitting in jail, that these calls were important. It was for the ones left behind in this quiet, empty house. That night, things felt calm, almost happy. Peaceful. Sheela was ready with the paratha filling when Gehna entered the kitchen, helping to knead the dough. Mother and daughter worked together, Sheela setting the saucer to make tea while Gehna prepared the parathas. Nandlal sat at the dining table, flipping through a stack of newspapers from the last few days, a poor attempt to reconnect with the outside world, filled with confusion and occasional surprise as he struggled in his own way.

Sheela brought the hot parathas, and Gehna followed with a bowl of green chutney.

Nandlal smiled, for the first time in a long while. He seemed at peace, even happy, as he reached for the water glass and asked for food. But Gehna knew it wasn't enough to stop him from drinking. Moments like these couldn't save him. There was always tomorrow—tomorrow that could ruin it all. Still, there was hope. They could live with hope, at least for now. But a whole decade of just hope? That was like hanging on by a thread with nothing to wait for.

After finishing her meal, Gehna retreated to her room. Her phone buzzed with a notification—the information about Gokesh's stay had been released. Without wasting time, she called Afzal.

"I was missing you," she said, her voice softening, taking on a seductive tone, trying to maintain his interest.

"What's with your voice? You don't have to do that. I like you for who you are." Afzal's response was calculated, trying to manipulate, but Gehna wasn't naive—she knew what he wanted.

"So, where are we meeting? Should I book a room?" His urgency wasn't lost on her, and she decided to set some terms.

"Ghana utavla hora hai re," Gehna teased, her tone sharp. "Seems like you're waiting for sex."

Afzal didn't flinch. "So what if I want sex? You want my help. I think we can help each other, find some common ground."

"You're right. But remember—every time you help me, you get one chance, just one shot." Gehna made her boundaries clear, and Afzal accepted, though his desperation was evident.

"So, when are we doing this? The kidnapping."

"In two days," Gehna replied, not wanting to delay any longer. She had already spent three days planning, and any further hold-up could complicate things.

"Before that, we need to be in Delhi. I'll come pick you up tomorrow. Be ready." Afzal cut the call abruptly, not wanting to linger on the line. He couldn't afford to be seen with the second phone at home. Any trace of suspicion would jeopardize the entire plan. While the kidnapping itself wasn't the difficult part, getting caught having an affair would be disastrous, potentially costing him his job. Afzal was confident about the kidnapping, but cheating? That was a different risk entirely.

The day passed, and the next morning, Gehna was ready. She had packed her bag and stepped out of the house, dressed in a saree. Afzal left his driver and drove his Scorpio to meet her at an intersection a little distance from her home and was visibly taken aback.

"Are we getting married or what?" he asked, seeing her in the traditional attire.

Gehna glanced down at herself, confused. "It's a saree. Am I turning you on? What's wrong?" she shot back, her tone playful, though she was slightly offended by the disgusted look on his face.

"We're about to drive 200 kilometers, and you're dressed for a cultural festival!" Afzal replied, exasperated.

Gehna felt embarrassed. He was right. She wanted to change immediately. "Give me five minutes," she muttered, stepping behind a tree. Quickly, she slipped out of the saree and changed into a tracksuit, stuffing the saree into her bag.

"Something's really wrong with you," Afzal sighed. "Don't you have any casual kurti or jeans? Something normal?"

"I'm a sarpanch," Gehna shot back. "I'm either dressed for an occasion or I'm in my room."

Afzal understood then. "Okay, fine. We'll go shopping as soon as we get to Delhi. Right now, you look like eye candy, and we need to blend you into the crowd." He tossed her bag into the back seat, and they sped off, leaving before anyone could see them together.

—

An uneasy silence hung between them, a reminder of how little they truly knew about each other. Despite having barely shared an afternoon together in the past decade, they had pieced together enough to grasp a basic understanding of one another's nature. Afzal had a sense that this kidnapping was tied to political maneuvering—he knew Gehna needed someone removed from the equation to execute a scheme, to manipulate a situation that would force an opponent to submit and lose the upcoming election.

Gehna, on the other hand, had a much clearer picture of Afzal's character. She knew him to be a predator, a man with multiple FIRs against him for molestation, attempted rape, and strong ties to the local criminal syndicate. Yet here he was, driving them to the city, taking care of her, not for any moral reason, but because of the sex he believed was owed to him. Not that it was ever owed—he just expected it. Despite the accusations and legal proceedings against him, Afzal still held a position of authority. Clearly, this was about more than just politics.

As she researched Parth's background, Gehna had come across articles that painted Afzal in a familiar, predatory light—a man who should have been detained long ago. She knew she needed to be cautious around him.

“You can take a nap in the back seat,” Afzal offered, lowering the volume on the radio and pointing to a pillow and blanket already laid out.

“You came prepared,” Gehna remarked, eyeing the setup with suspicion. It wasn’t hard to guess what was going through his mind.

"I have a wife and a kid, you know," Afzal added, sensing her wariness and feeling the need to explain himself.

"And yet, here you are, about to kidnap someone for a woman you’ve barely known for eight years," Gehna replied, keeping her gaze fixed on the road ahead.

"Yes, whatever you’re thinking is probably true. But don’t assume I’m getting anything out of this. This is a transaction," Afzal said defensively, uncomfortable with the judgment he felt in her tone. "But I’m the one being exploited in this scenario."

"And I’m kidnapping some random guy off the street," Gehna shot back. "So this isn’t exploitation. We’re both getting something out of this, just in different forms of payment. You want the guy, and I want you."

Afzal's reasoning was clear. The transaction wasn’t equal—she had the upper hand. When someone submits in exchange for something, they’re driven by their basic needs. Whether it’s hunger, shelter, or sex, it all comes down to primal instinct.

"Who is this guy, anyway? And why?" Afzal finally asked, needing to know the details to protect his own tracks.

"This won’t come back to you. Don’t worry," Gehna reassured him, having anticipated this question and prepared her response.

"That’s not the issue," Afzal said. "There are two of us in this. Me and you. You’re as involved as I am." He was confident that, as a woman, Gehna wouldn't be able to direct any blame toward him. For all he cared, Gehna could have been disposed of after the deed—but there was a title attached to her. She was under his jurisdiction, and any fallout would eventually affect his position as Superintendent of Police. If there was one thing Afzal had learned from his past actions, it was that no matter what you do, you bury it deep with anonymity.

"You're the Superintendent of Police," Gehna said, a hint of challenge in her voice, "You tell me what kind of criminal I have." She paused, considering how much to reveal. She thought about spinning a story, but she knew she needed him to stay involved until the end. Lying to him would be a mistake.

"At first, I figured this was about political rivalry," Afzal mused. "You're kidnapping someone's son to make a point; to show what might happen if the wrong person wins the election. But I don't think your village is connected enough to Delhi or anywhere else for someone over there to pose that big a threat to you."

He was right. It would be ridiculous to claim she was kidnapping someone's son just to win an election.

"Don't think too much about it. You give me this, I give you this," Gehna said, her voice steady caressing her hands over her body while grabbing her own breasts. Afzal couldn't object to this condition and line of reasoning, and knew he doesn't have to get any deeper into her matters as long as he's satisfied and getting what he wants.

The oppressive heat of the summer afternoon was seeping through the windshield, making it hard for Gehna to stay awake. Slowly, her eyes grew heavy, and she drifted off.

Suddenly, Afzal honked the horn on the empty highway, startling Gehna awake. She looked around, confused.

"If you're going to sleep, get in the backseat," Afzal said with a predatory grin. "I can't touch you while I'm driving."

His words sent a chill through her, confirming that he was far from the comforting or safe figure she needed. But she climbed into the backseat anyway, pulling the blanket over herself to rest.

"Don't..." she muttered with her eyes closed, sensing him adjusting the rear view mirror to watch her sleep. Afzal chuckled softly to himself and turned his attention back to the road.

Gehna didn't lie down to nap—she just wanted to avoid any conversation. The less they understood each other, the smoother the deal would go. So she stayed silent and still until they reached Delhi.

As they entered Gurgaon, Gehna stretched and yawned herself awake, sliding back into the seat beside Afzal. She gazed out the window at the bustling streets, watching people dressed in suits hurrying by, faces glued to their smartphones, waiting for cabs. Women wore outfits she'd only ever seen in movies or advertisements. The lifestyle she observed was one free from the restrictions that bound her. This city—so different from her world—was a place where everyone seemed liberated, while she remained tethered to tradition.

The deeper they went into Delhi, the more awkward she felt. The women's clothes grew skimpier, and imagining herself in such outfits made her uncomfortable. By the time they entered a mall, Gehna was hyper-aware of her own appearance. Her tracksuit felt glaringly out of place, and every glance from passing men felt like silent judgment.

"This is why you need better clothes," Afzal remarked, snapping her back to the moment. She looked at him and saw that his attire matched the city's polished style. He had adapted to this lifestyle, something she couldn't yet fathom. Gehna felt overwhelmed, wanting to leave the city that seemed to judge her with every step. The middle-aged women around her, confidently wearing fitted clothes, made her feel even smaller.

The mall was brightly lit, filled with scents from the shops, and buzzing with activity. Gehna knew this wasn't the real hurdle she faced. This was just another thing she had to push through. As they wandered through various stores, she tried on clothes, filling her basket while keeping her distance from Afzal. She didn't want him too close, but at the same time, she didn't want to feel lost in this unfamiliar place.

Then came the most uncomfortable part—buying underwear. She dreaded it. The thought of stepping into a store filled with bright, seductive displays of lingerie made her stomach churn. It felt humiliating to imagine walking out with a bag of bras and underwear, as other women did so casually.

Gehna asked Afzal to wait outside as she hurried into the store. "Good evening, ma'am. Would you like to try our seamless collection? They're light as a feather with smooth designs," the salesgirl chirped. Gehna froze for a moment, unable to make sense of the fancy pitch. The salesgirl, however, took one look at her and immediately seemed to size her up—perhaps deciding she wasn't a typical customer for this upscale boutique. Her first instinct was to guide Gehna out, assuming she couldn't afford the luxury brand, but Gehna wasn't done yet.

"Maaf kijiyega, kya mein aapko hamara naya collection dikha sakti hun? Yeh sab seamless designs hain—jo aap kisi bhi dress ke neeche pehnein, aapko wrinkles ya lines nahi dikhengi. Aur they're the most comfortable. I mean, sabse zyada—"

"Toh baaki sab comfortable nahin hai?" Gehna interrupted, curious but also completely clueless. She'd lost track of what she was asking.

"Uh, ma'am… Yeh naya collection exclusive hai, but these are better—fabric quality, material ka weight—"

"Andar hi toh pehenna hai... kya 10-20 kilo ki toh hogi nahin," Gehna said, completely missing the point. Her comment visibly irritated the salesgirl, who seemed ready to snap and drag her out of the store. But Gehna quickly picked up a set of three from the premium launch and said, "I'll take these."

The salesgirl calmed down a little, relieved to move the process along. They headed for the billing counter.

"I need a few bras as well," Gehna suddenly shouted, turning back to the racks while still in line. "Please, mein ek minute mein aari hun, yeh jagah kisi ko mat dena," she told the woman standing behind her, flashing an awkward smile. The woman chuckled and nodded as Gehna rushed off.

Nervous, Gehna grabbed a handful of bras without even checking the sizes, hurrying back to the line. When the bill flashed on the screen, she blinked in shock. It was much more than she'd anticipated, and she couldn't help but think of all the things she could've bought with the same amount back home. It felt like she'd just been swindled.

Out of the corner of her eye, she saw Afzal standing outside, watching her with a grin—not a friendly one, but the kind that sent a shiver down her spine. It was a smile that made her discomfort rise, confirming what she'd been trying to brush off.

She's spent it all on just appearance, just to blend in with the crowd of the capital city. For her presence to feel natural and not something absurd for anybody to find odd in any corner of the city. They bought the right attire, not just for one occasion as understood by Gehna.

The accommodation for both having separate rooms were arranged in a local hotel with no identification proof necessary arranged by Afzal's contacts. These were the things that Gehna couldn't have arranged for herself; eventually, she'd been caught if she were alone. But to be secured by the law to this extent, she needed someone like Afzal to be around. Initially, Afzal was supposed to be the fall guy for the actions, but in current circumstances, he was the invisibility cloak for her to pass through any security or situation.

—

Once they arrived, Gehna stepped out of the car, stretching her back. Afzal, still sitting in the driver's seat, called after her, "Get back inside." She hesitated but eventually slid back into the co-pilot seat, feeling uncomfortable. The stale smell of tobacco and alcohol in the car, which she had tolerated all the way to Delhi, was beginning to overwhelm her. The car had now become her second home, a space she'd have to endure for the next few days.

"What?" she asked, trying to understand his urgency.

"If you want to be famous, go ahead and get out. But we're here to kidnap someone, not do a ramp walk." Afzal's words were blunt, but they were exactly the kind of reality check she needed. This wasn't her world—the glamorous city and the bustling streets were new to her—but she was here on a mission, and she had to get used to the business of kidnapping, no matter how surreal it felt.

"Right," she muttered, processing the situation. "But won't it look suspicious with both of us just sitting here in a Scorpio? In the middle of Delhi?" She glanced around, suddenly aware of something that had seemed so obvious now. "Nobody drives a Scorpio in this city."

Afzal smirked. "This is a police vehicle. No one will dare look our way, trust me." He wasn't wrong. As Gehna scanned the surroundings, she realized that people were indeed keeping their distance, giving the bulky, official-looking car a wide berth. It was true—half car, half threat, no one would risk getting close.

"He might show up in an hour," Gehna said, showing Afzal a downloaded image of their target—a passport-sized photo, just clear enough for Afzal to recognize him. They waited in the car until the man eventually emerged from the hotel and got into a waiting cab.

"Where are we going?" Afzal asked, glancing over at her for direction.

"He's booked at Le Siempre. He'll leave around 3 for an event, so we need to get him before that." Gehna quickly pulled up the hotel's location on her phone, swiping through maps and setting up navigation. Afzal caught this, impressed for a moment, and flashed a brief smile as they drove towards the hotel.

"Now, This is what we'll do, you go inside, and ask the reception to inform Parth, that the cab from the event has arrived." Afzal turned to her and briefed her on the plan he's made.

"But, it's 2:30..."

"We can't afford to face the actual cab from the event. You go inside and get him outside, I'll bring in the gypsy. Now go." Gehna immediately stepped out, walking her way to the reception and asking for Vishwa Gokesh. Meanwhile, Afzal parked on an isolated street, changed the number plate, and added a little disguise to his looks—a slight touch of beard and an artificial tan rubbed on his skin to appear darker, putting a pan in his mouth. He waited for Vishwa Gokesh to arrive outside.

"We're coming outside" Afzal moved after the call, with the police ID to check in the drive-through and pick up both of them.

"Shor, bodhiya lagre hian, hum tumko chef li pucha dega. Tension nakko" Afzal changed his tone, but the real effect was done by the pan—it added texture to his voice. Vishwa Gokesh was a little bit suspicious, but nobody's ever been suspicious of stupid people, so he dropped his guards.

As soon as he settled in, before he could react, a hand clamped tightly around his neck, and another pressed a chloroform-soaked handkerchief against his face. He struggled, his eyes wide in shock, but within moments, his vision blurred. The last thing he saw was Gehna's smiling face before everything went dark.

"This was easy," he heard faintly as he slipped into unconsciousness.

Gokesh woke up groggy and disoriented, lying on a heap of hay in what seemed like an abandoned structure. The walls were bare, the roof missing, and irrigation channels crisscrossed the muddy floor. He cursed under his breath as the reality of his situation hit him. "Fuck!" he muttered, trying to sit up, but his legs felt strange—tingling. He glanced down and realized they were chained, tethered to an iron hook likely used for livestock.

His body still sluggish from the lingering effects of the chloroform, he scanned the space around him. No water, no supplies. Just him and four walls in the middle of nowhere. He leaned back against the rough stone wall, frustration and fear sinking in as the weight of the situation settled on him.

Chapter - 5

THE BANDIT QUEEN

Lying on the cold, unforgiving ground, Anand's senses slowly began to return, his body tingling with new awareness. He flexed his fingers, testing the strength in his hands, before finding his grip on the rough earth beneath him. With a groan, he pushed himself upright, his muscles aching with the strain. As he stood, his eyes darted around the room, searching desperately for anything that could help him escape this barren, isolated space. Four walls held him captive, their presence closing in like silent sentinels. His gaze fell on a few old Indian-style toilets, a hand pump, and some small buckets—pitiful reminders of basic needs, a way to pass the time. The place smelled faintly of livestock—it had probably been a cow shelter once.

"Arre koi hai, bachaoooo!" He screamed a couple times before he realized that there was a reason he was here. The place must be isolated.

Anand attempted to climb the walls, but the heavy chains around his ankles tugged him back, their cold bite limiting his freedom. He was free enough to relieve himself, to survive the day's most humiliating tasks, but food? There was nothing to eat. His stomach grumbled, empty, gnawing at him.

The scorching summer sun beat down relentlessly, turning the air into a stifling blanket of heat. Anand sought refuge in a shadowed corner, his body already dehydrated and weary. His mouth was parched, his head light, and he could feel the pull of unconsciousness creeping in, threatening to take him if he didn't drink soon. He spent the day shifting from corner to corner, chasing what little shade the prison-like room offered. It wasn't unfamiliar to him, this life of discomfort. Growing up in a modest household, he was no stranger to hardship—sharing meals, huddling under the same fan, enduring nights lit only by the stars during power cuts.

Yet, as he sat there, trapped, his mind raced. What was the purpose behind this kidnapping? He wasn't rich, not by any means. His family had nothing of significant value—his mother's small collection of jewelry, his father's modest earnings from playing matches. There was no wealth to ransom, nothing to leverage.

As the evening descended, the heavy iron gate screeched open, the sound of metal grinding against metal echoing through the room. Anand's heart skipped a beat, his body tensing instinctively. A woman stepped inside. Her presence commanded attention—Gehna. She moved with purpose, carrying a bottle of water and several polythene bags filled with food—curry, chapatis, and rice. The simple scent of the meal was enough to make Anand's stomach twist painfully in hunger. Gehna placed the food aside and sat across from him, maintaining a deliberate distance. Her eyes were cold, calculating, as they locked onto his.

"I want someone out of jail, and you're going to help me do that." Her voice was low, steady, and without emotion. The statement hung in the air between them, blunt and unapologetic.

Anand tried to speak, his voice hoarse from thirst. "I think you've got the wrong guy. I'm—"

"Anandparth, Anand," Gehna interrupted, her eyes narrowing slightly. "You're a grandmaster, well-known for maintaining your rank in the world of chess. You're not rich, so paying a ransom isn't an option. I know all of this already. But you," she said, her lips curving ever so slightly, "are exactly what I need." Her words sent a chill down his spine. She leaned back, her expression unreadable, and pulled out a packet of *Beedi* and matchstick to light it up.

"I can't..."

Gehna's voice was low, seething, as she stormed toward him. Her hand shot out, grabbing a fistful of his hair, yanking his head down, and slamming it hard into the sand. His face was pressed against the scorching ground, grit and heat making every breath a struggle. As he tried to raise his arms, groping blindly for her wrist, her grip only tightened, fingers like steel, impossible to shake. With one swift pull, she hoisted him back up, forcing him to look at her.

"Look at me!" she ordered, her voice cutting through the haze around him. She slapped him, once, twice, her heavy blows marking his face, leaving stinging red streaks across his cheeks, and he felt blood starting to trickle from his nose. The pain jolted through him, sharp and sudden, just as she held up a burning beedi, pressing it against his forehead. He gasped, his whole body jolting as he felt the burn sear into his skin.

"Saale kuposhit..." she sneered, as he trembled beneath her grip, pinned down by her rage and strength.

Without breaking her focus, Gehna slipped her hand into her pocket, her fingers curling around the cold, heavy weight of her revolver. In one swift movement, she raised it, aiming directly at his leg. The gunshot rang out, close enough to graze his skin—close enough to send his heart racing. The bang echoed through the small space, and Anand flinched as the bullet struck the ground mere inches from him.

She didn't flinch, bringing the hot muzzle to his mouth, pressing it against his tongue, searing him with its heat.

"Teri iron ki kami poori karne mein mint ka time ni lagna mujhe," she spat, her voice a calm, deadly whisper.

"If I kill you, you'll become the tragic headline: 'A brilliant mind, lost too soon.' You're more useful to me alive, for now. So eat," she added, gesturing toward the food she'd brought with a dismissive wave. "Then, choose."

She turned on her heel and left the room, leaving the gate wide open behind her. Anand stared at the polythene bags. It was degrading, humiliating, but his hunger gnawed at him with a ferocity he couldn't ignore. Slowly, and painfully, he crawled towards the food, his pride swallowed by his primal need to survive.

Minutes passed, and Gehna returned with a bottle of water in her hand. She stood still, watching as Anand struggled, unable to reach the food. Their eyes met again, a silent exchange passing between them. She stepped closer, stopping just out of his reach, savoring the control she had over him. Without a word, she picked up the food and tossed it toward him, the bags landing haphazardly near his outstretched hand.

"I'll help you," Anand rasped. "I'll do whatever you need. I'll try. I'm just a chess player, but I'll do my best to help." His voice was raw with desperation.

Gehna's expression didn't change. She stood there, staring down at him, her gaze hard and unwavering. Then, without a word, she turned and left once again.

Hours later, sitting in her jeep, Gehna received a call from Afzal. His voice was eager, hungry.

"I'd like to redeem my prize," Afzal said, the words heavy with anticipation.

Gehna's heart quickened, but she remained composed. "Where and when?" she asked, her tone steady.

"Come to my farmhouse. I'll send the location. Come fast, I'm waiting."

Gehna knew exactly what this meant. She had prepared herself for this, long before the kidnapping had even taken place. There were no illusions in her mind about what she had agreed to, what she had to endure to ensure her brother's safety. She had steeled herself for the cuts, the bruises and the bites. She had been living in a constant state of danger for years, and this was just another part of the price she had to pay.

The farmhouse was secluded, surrounded by police guards and surveillance. It felt like a fortress, but it also felt like a trap. As she stepped inside with a mask on to cover her face, with a bag carrying an extra pair of clothes, her eyes found Afzal, walking around naked like he owned the place—and her. The sight made her stomach twist, but she stayed calm and composed. She took a seat, trying to keep as much distance between them as possible. But Afzal had other plans. He moved closer, his presence overwhelming. He grabbed her, pulling her into his arms, his hand roughly yanking away her dupatta. His fingers brushed against her chest, tracing the curve of her breasts through the thin fabric of her suit.

"You are mine, now," he whispered, his breath hot against her cheek. His tongue flicked out, licking her skin, tasting the sweat on her.

A shiver of revulsion ran through her, but she forced herself to remain still. This was part of the deal. She had to endure it.

"Salty," Afzal murmured, his tongue licking against her neck. "But I like it."

She stepped back, her eyes roaming over her body. "Is this little show just for me?" she asked with eyes filled with disgust. "Or do you walk around your house like this for your kids too?"

Afzal's hand gripped her butt, pulling her toward a table covered in whiskey bottles. "Make me a drink," he ordered, his voice thick with desire.

Gehna didn't hesitate. She grabbed a bottle and smashed it against the wall, the glass shattering in an explosion of sound. "I'm not your slave," she said, her voice cold. "I'm here to repay a debt, nothing more. So don't expect me to play your little games."

Afzal laughed, the sound low and rumbling. He stepped closer, his face inches from hers. "You're right," he said softly, his voice dripping with mock sincerity. "You. Are. Right."

Their eyes met, the tension between them thick and electric. "Let's get to it…" Afzal turned her around facing the kitchen and with a small knife in his hands ripped the suit off of her, cutting the strips off of her bra, and slid the knife between her ass, cutting off her underwear.

He rubs his dicks against her ass, pouring whiskey on her backs and licking it as it runs down.

"One shot, you said," Afzal's voice slithered through the air, his fingers cold as they trailed down Gehna's back and curved their way to her chest, slipping beneath the fabric, teasing the soft hair on her bosom. His touch was rough and demanding. She could feel the weight of it against her skin, making her stomach tighten with unease. He rubbed her with a brutal impatience running fingers around her pubic hair, his eyes gleaming with the thrill of control. "You'd want more if we went for it. Let's play this game."

Gehna had never felt a man's touch before, and now, her body trembled—not with desire, but with the sickening awareness that this was not how she had ever imagined her first intimate experience. This was Afzal—cruel, domineering, and nothing like the lover she would have chosen. But she was trapped, her body betraying her with unfamiliar sensations as her mind screamed for escape.

"Go to the bedroom," he ordered, slapping her butt with a force that stung, leaving a burning imprint on her skin. Gehna flinched, shame flooding through her as she stumbled toward the dimly lit room. The air was thick with the sweet, suffocating scent of candles, and neon lights flickered ominously from the corners, casting distorted shadows. There was no air conditioning, the room stifling as her skin prickled under the oppressive heat.

From the other side of the door, she could hear him rummaging furiously through drawers, his voice rising in frustration. "Rama! Where are my pills?" His shout was followed by the sound of slaps—a few hard, loud smacks as he punished his helper for failing to meet his demands. Gehna stood frozen, mostly naked, clutching her discarded clothes against her body in a futile attempt to hide herself. The walls seemed to mock her, reflecting her humiliation back at her.

"Stop it," she whispered to herself, her voice breaking. With a sudden surge of anger, she flung the clothes away and lay down on the bed, her body stiff, her mind detached from the nightmare unfolding around her.

Afzal entered, his eyes dark with lust. He moved quickly, yanking her leg toward him, his mouth descending on her body with animalistic hunger. He kissed and licked every inch of her skin, his hands rough as they explored her, his teeth grazing her flesh, leaving marks as though claiming ownership. His hard cock pressed against her, rubbing against the thick hair between her legs, the sensation alien and unwanted. He moved upward, his mouth finding her firm, pointed nipples, biting and sucking with a ferocity that made her wince. Each kiss, each mark he left behind, felt like another piece of her slipping away.

She lay motionless, staring blankly at the ceiling, her eyes fixed on the fan that stood still, turned off. She tried to focus on anything but him—anything but the sickening weight of his body pressed against hers, his hands groping, and his breath hot against her skin.

Afzal fumbled with a condom, the dim light making it difficult for him to put it on. He cursed under his breath, struggling. "Fuck this," he muttered, throwing the condom aside in frustration. He grabbed Gehna roughly, pulling her closer, his fingers digging into her thighs as he positioned himself.

"No, this isn't what we agreed to," Gehna said, her voice rising in panic as she realized what he intended. "No!" she shouted, her voice sharp and angry.

Afzal, enraged by her defiance, tore open another condom and put it on with a furious smile. His eyes gleamed with a sick satisfaction as he pinned her down, his breath coming in heavy pants. He leaned over her, his face inches from hers, his lips curling into a sneer as he pushed against her, trying to force his way in.

But his body betrayed him. Just as he began to enter, he gasped, his body tensing, and then suddenly, he climaxed. It was over in a flash—a pathetic, anticlimactic end to the violence he had been so desperate to inflict.

Gehna felt the shift immediately. She grabbed his softening penis with her hand, holding it with a tight grip as she looked up at him. "You're done," she said, her voice cold, her heart pounding with a strange sense of triumph.

Afzal's eyes widened in shock, his body trembling as the reality of his failure sank in. "No, this can't be," he stammered, looking down at himself, his face contorted with disbelief. "I haven't done anything," he shouted, his voice cracking.

"You've done enough," Gehna replied icily, her words cutting through the air like a knife. She pushed him away, her mind clear and focused now. She had more to protect than just herself. This wasn't over.

Without another word, she grabbed her bag, quickly pulling on the spare clothes she had brought with her. Afzal was still reeling, muttering to himself in disbelief, but Gehna didn't look back. "It's not my fault," he mumbled weakly. "I behaved."

She shot him a final, scornful glance as she adjusted her clothes. "You've done enough," she repeated, her voice sharp as she revealed the bruises, the bite marks, the angry red scratches he had left on her skin.

"I'm leaving," she said, her voice steady with resolve as she slipped on her sandals and stormed out of the house, her body aching but her spirit unbroken. The eyes of the police guards followed her as she marched toward her jeep, but she kept her head high, ignoring their judgment behind her mask, their silent accusations.

After half an hour, her phone rang. It was Afzal. She answered, his voice furious on the other end.

"Come back, right now!" he's grunting, angered yet drunk to a cause.

"I won't," she replied calmly. "We had a deal. I respected my side of it. It's your problem if you can't last a single round." Her words struck like a hammer, obliterating what was left of his fragile ego. His scream of frustration echoed through the phone before the line went dead.

Gehna exhaled, her chest heaving with the weight of the day. She started the engine, driving away as the setting sun dipped below the horizon, casting long shadows over the narrow village lanes. As she rode through, villagers greeted her warmly, unaware of the storm she had just weathered. The children ran to her, smiling, their innocence a painful contrast to the darkness she carried inside.

"Betti, tu theek toh hai?" one of the elders asked, concern etched on his weathered face.

Gehna smiled faintly, her face hidden behind a dupatta, her body fully covered in long sleeves, concealing the evidence of her shame. "Thand lag rahi hai, Taau," she said lightly, keeping her voice steady as she gently avoided placing a hand on the child's head for a blessing.

"Padho, likho, ache aadmi bano," she murmured to the children, her voice soft as she stepped back into her jeep. Tears pricked her eyes, and as she drove away, leaving the village behind, she let them fall—silent witnesses to the pain she could never share.

—

The Jeep stopped beside the local *dhaba.*

"Chacha! Ek thaali baandh dio zara. Bhookh si laagri hai," she shouted.

"Thaari maa ne aaj khana na banaya ke?" the man behind the counter shouted back, and with no response, he started frying the dal and packed a few chapatis, some rice and some other curries and salad.

She takes them and storms into the fields to the guy at the brink of his hunger.

—

Anand was sitting quietly looking at the chess board he's carved in the soaked sand, with pieces marked in different boxes.

"Han bhyi, chess master."

Gehna entered the scene keeping her distance with the revolver stuck to her sides. She throws the food in his lap.

"I'm in. I'll do it, but I have some conditions. Not like conditions but ideas."

Gehna sat there silently waiting for him to speak further.

"One, Nobody dies. I mean nobody." Gehna nods to it.

"Second, I want a chess board." Gehna turns to the carved out chess board and accepts it even if she couldn't understand the requirement.

"Third, I'm about to do a lot. Everything leads me to either death by you, or jail. And I don't want either of them. When we're done,

I want out and we won't talk about it ever again." Gehna nods because all these demands were not demands but what she wanted all along, even though leaving him alive in the world would be a liability and a constant threat of her getting caught but she agreed.

"Fourth…"

"That's it." Gehna says it and pulls out the revolver from her side.

"You don't need to threaten anymore, I'm on your side." Anand rests his back against the wall and sits there opening the pack of food.

"I won't make unnecessary demands, and won't try to escape." Gehna looked around but there wasn't a single hole in the wall for him to look around and expect some help. And he was making sense and seemed like he would not resist a lot.

"But if you did try, and successfully left this place. The next time I find you, I'll shoot you—with every bullet I have. And I'll make sure it's painful." Gehna said and left the scene. Finally to her home,

Stepping into her home, she found her father, sitting on the dinner table with newspaper in his hands, and her mother whipping the dining table with her usual table cloth. She turned to Gehna and said, "Ja naha le, khaana laga deti hun." Gehna nodded so as to not burst into tears and took the stairs to her room and laid down on her bed for a while. Went for the bath, furiously running her whole body, being reminded of every lick, every ick she felt through those hours. She kept rubbing herself till her skin was red because of the pressure it felt. It was better, these burns felt much better.

—

The power cut had left the night pitch dark and unbearably stifling, robbing Gehna of sleep as she lay in bed, haunted by half-formed shadows of nightmares that wouldn't let her rest. By morning, she felt a strange calm, her focus sharpened with a quiet ferocity. She made her way into the market, eyeing shelves until she found a chessboard—one with hand-carved wooden pieces instead of cheap plastic. She traced the smooth edge of the box, finding comfort in its weight. "Pack this one," she murmured to the shopkeeper, before heading out to the barren outskirts where Anand was being kept.

"Oh, the queen is back," Anand muttered as she approached, his voice rasping from the corner where he sat, leaning against the rough wall with a small trench dug beneath him for makeshift comfort. His smirk held a glint of something dark as his eyes flitted to the board she held.

"We're getting straight to it," Gehna replied coolly, tossing him the chessboard. He opened it, a little too eagerly, sliding the pieces onto the board with precision, arranging them with a practiced hand.

"Alright, I need to see the route…" Anand's voice was low but insistent as he arranged the pieces on the board with careful precision.

"We're not going anywhere…"

"I NEED it," he snapped, turning to Gehna, his face set.

"Why?" she pressed, crossing her arms.

"To set things up," he replied, his voice carrying a hint of impatience.

Gehna's gaze narrowed. "I don't want bits and pieces, Anand. Breathe, and tell me what's actually in your head." Agitated, she picked up a nearby stone and tossed it in his direction, the sharp sound snapping him out of his focus.

"Alright, alright. Listen," he sighed, rubbing his forehead before leaning back over the board.

The scene on the board was stark: only a black queen and bishop on one side, while the other side showed a lone black pawn where the king should've been surrounded by the white pieces all over.

"We're going to need more than just you, me, and that cop behind the wheel. If he's in on it," Anand said, placing a rook beside the queen with a deliberate motion, "then I need someone with skill. I mean, serious skill. We're talking people with near-military training, maybe even high-level athletes." He paused, his fingers hovering over the rook as if weighing options, spinning it once before setting it back down.

"Oh, I'm going to need more than just a few things—the police van, and I need to see the entire route," Anand said, his voice steady but with an edge that made his determination clear.

Gehna, who initially felt a wave of reluctance at his demands, took a moment to process. It was clear now: he needed every potential complication accounted for, every factor laid out. One missed detail, and this plan could mean the death of any one of them.

"Fine. I'll get you the jail van. But you're staying right here. No driving out on the road."

"Hmm… don't take me out there, show me the map. I'll lay out the possible route, and you go out there and record the tolls, the shops along the way, and anything nearby—from roadsides to the markets they'd likely cross." Anand extended a hand for her phone. Gehna hesitated, her eyes narrowing slightly, but eventually held it out, maintaining her grip and stance, with one hand still resting on her revolver, just in case.

Focused, Anand dove into the maps, searching for a route that wouldn't need excessive security, one where the typical guard contingent might be kept to a minimum. He muttered as he zoomed in and out on the screen, pointing to routes circling interstate boundaries, especially towards those connecting to expressways. "Madhya Pradesh," he whispered, his finger tracing the towns and expressways between Bhundsi Jail and the central prison in Madhya Pradesh, noting every toll booth, each intersection.

"Your brother's transfer request needs to be re-routed to Madhya Pradesh's central jail." He took screenshots, his concentration unwavering. "This phone of yours—it isn't registered anywhere, right?" He glanced at her, almost in a whisper.

"No, not registered and never linked. Now, give it back." Her voice was cold, but Anand was too engrossed to take notice. When he finally looked up, he froze, realizing she had the revolver aimed squarely at his head.

"Alright, alright, I was just curious." He forced a shaky laugh, handing her the phone.

"And don't forget the jail van," Gehna muttered as she prepared to leave. Just then, she caught herself thinking about who to call to make these arrangements. Almost instinctively, she grimaced as her mind landed on Afzal. Just as she considered it, his ringtone filled the air—his phone was buzzing with a tune so corny, she cringed.

"Haan, bol," Afzal's voice was thick with a pout; clearly still irked that she hadn't answered his calls.

"I need a police bus," she said coolly, though irritation tickled the edge of her voice.

"You know where to find me," Afzal retorted, his tone laden with innuendo.

"No, not right now. And don't talk to me like that," she snapped.

"Like what? You left me there, and you didn't hold up your end of the deal." His tone was accusatory, laced with unforgettable irritation.

"Afzal, honestly, I don't mean to insult your manhood but, *puura chaat kharoch ke TU jhad gaya toh isme meri kya galti ha?* I was there, waiting, and you dropped the ball. Next time, maybe bring your A-game," she said with a sardonic chuckle, her jaw clenched tight.

"Alright, alright, but when are you coming, then?"

"Hold your horses. First, get me a van and a Gypsy. I'll come by and pick them up." She could almost see him rolling his eyes.

"Got a couple at the farmhouse. Just leave the plates," he replied, as if to assure her of another chance.

With that, Gehna hung up and leaned back in her seat, parking the jeep by the side of the road, letting the seat recline as she exhaled. For a moment, the ceiling of the jeep was her entire world as she shut her eyes, forcing her mind to silence.

—

The next day, Anand stood chained to the ground, his eyes scanning the interiors of the police van, noting every console, the radio, and intercom setup. "Mind if I get a few photos?" he asked, his voice even.

"Sure, I'll get that," Gehna replied, snapping a few shots with her phone before tucking it safely back into her pocket.

"Now here's abing task for you, I need to see the route. And for that, you need to do one thing."

Gehna waited for the instructions.

"You're being harassed by a M.P, member of parliament,"

"I know what M.P is…"

"Okay Instruction number one: This person calls you on random hours to withdraw her stand from coming elections with threats of killing her family. You go and tell this to your brother. Then you ask him what to do, and that you don't want your family to get involved in this. Then specifically tell him to not do anything about it, or get involved."

Gehna had a limited understanding of where this could lead, but she actually doesn't want her brother to get involved in these kinds of things anymore. If she could, she'd have done it all by herself—but a single brick can lay the foundation, but it can't be the bridge.

"Why do you want him to do something? Tell me everything." Gehna asks further to understand the gravity of the situation and keep things in control if push came to shove.

"Just do that."

Gehna left immediately, jumping in her car as she dialed a video call to her brother. While the call was dialing, she smudged her kajal a bit and tidied up her hair slightly, trying to keep the stress and heaviness in her voice visible through her appearance.

"Ke kar raha hai, chhote." Gehna smiled, looking at her brother. She could see in his eyes how much he had changed over the time.

"Ghaans kaat ke aaye hain abhi, raat kitaab uthai hai, ek library se. Vahi padhunga." Deepak kept looking at his phone screen, he spotted what was planted there for him to see. "Kanghi kar leti, jinaavar laagri hai kasam se. Aise na nikaliye ghar se." Gehna chuckled a bit before her face went stiff.

"Tell me, now." Deepak's face dropped, and now he was seriously invested.

"There's an MLA or MP in Madhya Pradesh. Actually, leave it, it's just politics, I can handle it."

"The least you can do is tell me, it's not like I'm there to fight your battles," Deepak wants to hear, as this is something which puts a visible strain on his sister's life.

"He's calling me at odd hours, mostly threat calls, about..." Gehna paused for a while, looking at Deepak, wiping his face with his hands, trying to cover his anger.

"Killing my family, so. I just wanted to know if you're safe."

"Don't worry too much about it. What's his name and number? I'll take care of it."

"No, you're not getting involved in this. You're in jail, if you forgot." Morally, she was not willing to stake his clean record over the past decade of imprisonment. It was too big of a risk to get him out of there. *What if the plan doesn't work?* This wasn't something she could afford to think about right then. She needed everything to succeed. Despite the instructions coming from Anand, this sounded right.

"I'm not. Trust me." Deepak said with a straight face.

"Breaking news: There was an attempted assasination on Sambhal Shrivastava, an MP from Madhya pradesh. Our correspondent has confirmed that Sambhal Shrivastava was mildly bruised by the bullet scratching around his chin crossing the ear but the shock nearly took his hearing. If the bullet or he were slightly closer, it'd have been a tragic incident. The responsibility of the attempt has been taken by Raghuram, a convicted criminal in Bhundsi jail. The shooter was a hired goon but the next attempt will not be a fake, as said by Raghuram. Moving on to…" The news broadcast of the incident covered another name but Gehna understood who's behind all this. She woke up and rushed back to her jeep, getting back to Anand.

"So now you will need three cars, and six dashcams. I want all three of them to chase the route police take to get Raghuram from bhundsi jail to crossing MP borders. I want the shops, toll, stops and every intersection they pass through." Barely awake, Gehna hadn't spoken a word, but Anand knew what had happened and had already prepared his steps further. If things are unfolding as he has planned, then there was less to worry about.

"Okay, consider it done."

"Now, there's one important person we need for this to go smoothly. You NEED a sniper."

He placed the rook with exaggerated precision, encircling the lone pawn against the fleet of white. He glanced up at her.

“What’s the plan?” she asked with her voice low but insistent. Her patience was thin, her foot tapping on the gritty ground.

"I thought we agreed—no killing." But at times, the tone, the words he say, go beyond challenging her, trying to dominate her decisions.

"We did," Anand replied, still absorbed in his planning. "Shots only to disable—tires, cameras, legs if necessary."

"When do you need this sniper?"

"When are you planning the jailbreak?" he asked, his tone almost casual.

"Yesterday," she replied, unbothered.

"Then you need three more people—not just a sniper, but someone skilled in hand-to-hand combat and another who can run. I won't tell you how to pull this off, but that’s what it’ll require."

"This needs to be discreet, and you're just adding things to the list." Gehna grabbed Anand by his hair, the tension snapping through her voice.

"Shopping, par nikla, hai. Yeh laado, voh laado," she muttered angrily, punctuating each word with a punch to his stomach, a slap across his face, leaving him teetering unsteadily.

"If you don't want to take the bullet, you need people," Anand panted, his voice strained, his gaze holding hers despite the pain. "I don't wanna die, and I don't wanna kill. There's an escape, and they'll be armed. How many bullets do you want in your chest? That's the question," he said, still hunched but studying her fiercely.

Then, with a surprising ease, his eyes flicked up to hers, his tone strangely casual. "Is there anything to eat?" he added, the faintest smirk lurking beneath the bruises.

She shot him a glare. “Do I look like your lunch lady?” Her voice was as cold as stone.

He patted the floor beside him, inviting her to sit, but she stayed rooted where she was. "Look at the board. What do you see?"

"Enough with the riddles," she hissed, her patience barely tethered. Her fingers twitched, her eyes fierce.

He pointed at the queen and bishop on the board. "All we have is you and me, with the cop as potential backup." He slid a rook onto the board. "Add a sniper, and we're three."

He turned his gaze to her, but she felt the simmering tension inside her boil over.

"We'll get him transferred," he said quietly, his voice steady, though the hint of blood on his temple glistened. "And take him then."

Gehna began to storm out but she paused, looking back over her shoulder. She found Anand looking at the black pawn surrounded by a few white pawns, facing the queen and bishop.

"If we somehow get him to move from the prison, we'll have a better possibility of getting him, with less, officials, and officers surrounding him." Gehna stood there as Anand took off his t-shirt to wipe the blood from his forehead. Her eyes were hard as she threw him a handkerchief.

"Cover it up," she commanded, without a flicker of concern in her gaze. He took it, dabbing the blood away as she turned on her heel and strode out into the unforgiving daylight, leaving him alone with the chessboard and his scattered thoughts.

"And for that, we need people. If we can't kill them, we distract them." Anand rushed his wound as he added a black rook, horse, and bishop in different boxes and moved the white pawns surrounding the black pawn to block the recently added black pieces. Leaving the black pawn piece alone, then he moves the queen piece and replaces it with a white pawn piece beside the black pawn.

"Sniper?" Gehna asks clenching her fists, understanding the meaning, and going back to Afzal. Anand nods. "I'll get you food tonight." Gehna dashed out of the scene in her jeep.

Chapter - 6

THE BULL'S EYE

Indulged in his chessboard, Anand was looking for possible chances and the routes he could use with an optimal kidnapping success. But however he looked at it, he was going to need more than one person to make it secure, with no deaths. No matter how you play it, you could never win without moves to spare, to find the best tactic. It's not hard to step in, you just need a little courage. But to walk out alive, it would take a serious skill in survival.

"But working with monkeys would be deadly."

—

Gehna stepped inside of her room and switched on her lights. She experienced the terror of the tidy room. Messed up clothes, and everything covered with the reminder of her last week's action in the form of fabrics of every kind. The fresh pair of dresses, and suits ridden with the odor of unwanted experiences and fragrance, blended with perfumes and chloroform laden handkerchief.

She needed to clean everything before anybody saw and began to question her state of mind. She couldn't let any of that be seen by her mother. Lying is something Gehna wanted to avoid as much as possible, because that was something she couldn't achieve in front of her mother.

Gehna laid a dupatta on the floor and dropped everything that needed washing. She bundled it up moving towards the washing machine. While dropping her clothes, she immediately realized about the handkerchief. She took it out to not leave the smell in her clothes. She dropped it in the bin. She was reminded of the hours she spent enduring a consensual attempt of rape, the price she was supposed to pay. Eventually it will leave it was going to print all over her life, but it's something she had to prepared herself for. It didn't happen the last time, but this time, he'll be cautious and he wouldn't go easy. Which reminded her of…

"I need a sniper now."

—

Afzal sat in quiet anticipation, waiting for the moment he knew would come. Gehna's voice, steady yet tinged with urgency, reached him over the phone.

"Umm… I need your help," she said.

He smirked slightly, a practiced expression that masked his true thoughts. "Where are we going this time?" He could have wrapped up the job by nightfall if he wanted, but this wasn't just about the task at hand. Gehna—sharp, determined, and still learning—needed a plan, and Afzal knew he had to be the one to craft it.

"Where he'll be, what he's supposed to be doing, his age, weight, whatever details you have. I know you won't give me the name," he continued.

"We're going to Chandigarh," she responded.

"I'll get the plates and lights."

"Hein, kyon?" she asked, caught off guard by the reference.

"Number plates, and police lights," Gehna smirked.

"So, do you have a plan?" Gehna's eyes met his, searching for assurance.

"Give me a day," Afzal replied, already piecing together ideas. "Tell me about him."

"He jogs, has a simple routine between home and office. No drugs, no alcohol. That's all," she said, revealing little more than a shadow of the man she was after. Afzal's mind churned, parsing through the vague description—there were thousands like that, a needle in a haystack.

"Okay," he sighed, "you're not gonna be much help, again."

"You give me what I want," she replied, eyes narrowing slightly.

"We will go tomorrow evening." There was no need for more discussion; he knew this was a chance he couldn't let slip.

"Tonight, after dinner. Meet me behind the temple and pack accordingly. We need to be back by tomorrow night," Gehna instructed firmly. The mention of dinner sparked something in her voice. Family dinners had become sacred to her—a sign that despite the chaos she stirred, she could keep things steady at home.

"Okay," Afzal said, hanging up. He didn't have to play by her rules, but the motivation—both hers and his own—pushed him onward. He recalled their last attempt, imperfect and seared into his memory. This time, he would do better.

Gehna placed her phone on charge, its glow fading as she turned towards the kitchen. The familiar scent of spices filled the air as she stepped inside to find her mother stirring a pot of kadhi.

"What's for dinner today?" Gehna asked, settling beside her.

"Kadhi," her mother replied. "Knead the dough for chapatis," she added, handing Gehna the thaali.

Gehna poured flour and water into the dish, mixing it slowly. "Maa…" she began, her voice softer now.

"Ji, bataiye," her mother responded without pausing, eyes focused on the simmering pot.

"You do everything for this family—cook, clean, even when you're not feeling well. Why?" Gehna's eyes searched her mother's face for an answer.

Her mother paused for a moment, then spoke, "It's not just about cooking. It's my love for this family, my commitment to your father. He's faced enough hardship—lost his parents before you were even born. I don't want him to feel alone."

"But what do you get out of it?" Gehna's fingers were still in the dough.

Her mother's smile was small but warm. "I get this," she said, gesturing to the humble scene around them. "A quiet moment, talking with you, no worries weighing me down." She covered the pot and began peeling carrots for the salad. "He gave me a safe space, and I made it a home—for both of us. Now go to him. He might start drinking if he's alone too long."

Gehna's smile mirrored her mother's as she nodded and left the kitchen.

Her father, Nandlal, sat at the dining table, a glass of whiskey in hand and the bottle within reach. He looked up as Gehna sat beside him, a hint of a grin playing on her lips.

"Hmm," he muttered, catching her pointed stare.

"I'll finish this one," he said, pushing the bottle away, then took a sip. Gehna folded her arms and rested her head on them, watching him.

"What do you want?" Nandlal asked, pretending to read the newspaper.

"Nothing," she replied, eyes never leaving his face.

"Then why are you here?" he grumbled, still not turning the page.

"Because I want to. Koi dikkat hai aapko?" A playful challenge hung in her words.

"Nahin," he muttered, his lips twitching with the ghost of a smile. He turned a page just as Gehna's mother arrived, placing steaming dishes on the table.

"Put that glass aside and eat," Sheela said sharply. Nandlal obeyed, setting the paper down as Gehna nudged the whiskey glass further away. With a resigned sigh, he began to eat, fingers reaching for the chapati.

"Haath dhoye aapne?" Sheela's voice cut through the room. He paused, then stood to wash his hands, a sheepish smile creeping onto his face. As he walked away, Gehna and her mother exchanged amused glances, breaking into quiet giggles.

—

The rhythmic shouts of the chai vendor, "Chai garam! Chai chai chaiyaa!" filled the air, weaving through the usual chaos of the trucks moving in and out of this *dhaba* swiftly into the night. *Chotu* hustled for a sale while drivers and families sought brief moments of distraction amid the journey. Some, lucky enough to have *Khaat*, and others adjusting themselves to chairs surrounding tables held together by aged and rusty iron nails..

A couple chairs, occupied by Gehna and Afzal, sat alone beside his government-registered jeep, with everyone isolating them both. The owner of the *dhaba* expected to be on his best behavior.

"What's the plan?" Gehna checks the taste and adds salt to the curries and in *raita*, her mind replaying every intense moment she'd shared with Afzal at the farmhouse. The confusion and emotions that followed still gnawed at her, a distracting presence that she couldn't shake off, especially with Afzal always nearby.

"There's already enough salt in that." Afzal pulled out a tube of sunblock. Gehna seemed puzzled.

"It's not for you; it's for him," Afzal responded.

"How are we doing it?" she pressed, urgency threading through her thoughts.

"In broad daylight, in the market. A guy collapses; we step in to help. Simple."

"What's in the sunscreen?" Gehna's brows furrowed, a hint of apprehension sparking.

"It absorbs into the skin quickly and has a drug that numbs and puts him to sleep," he explained.

"Like chloroform?"

"Yes, but custom-made. Lab-designed. Got it from an assassin for hire," Afzal's tone carried a casual confidence.

"Assassin?" Gehna's heart thudded at the word.

"Contract killer, sort of like your brother," Afzal mockingly stated, but found Gehna stopped midway of taking a bite, staring at him.

"But let's not dwell on that. We will keep it quiet and quick." Afzal slipped the tube into his pocket, awaiting her response.

"Eat," Gehna replied, cutting off the conversation as she resigned from reacting to anything after the remarks on his brother.

"Sorry." Afzal apologized, taking another bite.

"Hmm..." She said, with her mouth filled with the biggest bite ever.

The dim room of the cheap hotel was quiet, but Gehna's mind buzzed with thoughts. The stakes were high, and the weight of another kidnapping bore heavily upon her. She knew that if she were working alone, she'd have already been caught. Afzal was the reason she still had her freedom. His timely intervention had saved her, but it was now her task to ensure he stayed invested, satisfied, and willing to follow her lead. The stakes were higher than ever.

Her gaze flicked to the door, half-expecting a knock. When it finally came, it was soft, measured. "Are you awake?" Afzal's voice called, low but firm.

"What do you want?" she asked, a familiar wariness taking hold. To her, men all seemed to harbor the same desire. Yet, tonight felt different.

"Water," came his reply, unexpectedly polite.

"He's definitely not here for water," she thought but said nothing as she opened the door. Afzal stepped inside, his eyes sweeping over her wet hair and the fresh scent of her shower. She stood in a bathrobe, and he couldn't help the sheepish smile that flitted across his face.

"What?" she asked, her voice edged with suspicion.

"Kuch ni, Jaatni bhadiya laagri hai. Bahar na nikaliye, rape ho jaega," he muttered, his gaze softening. He reached for the bottle on the dresser, but as he did, he leaned in, brushing his lips against her cheek, trailing down her neck. A shiver raced down her spine.

Afzal's eyes narrowed as he sensed the tension crackling in the air outside Bulk-fit. The gym-goers and staff shifted uneasily under the hard gaze of the police vehicle parked right outside. The gym's manager, a wiry man with a neatly trimmed mustache, hesitated before approaching the jeep, trying to mask his apprehension with a polite smile. The morning sun cast sharp, unwavering shadows, highlighting the sweat beading on his brow.

"Hello, sir," the manager started, his voice shaky but courteous. "I'm really sorry, but some of our regulars are concerned about why a police jeep is stationed outside our gym. Is there anything I can assist you with?"

Afzal's dark eyes shifted to meet the manager's, assessing him with a calculated stare. He was dressed in casual attire—a faded T-shirt and jeans—but the heavy beard, rough complexion, and the faint tan made him seem imposing. The mole, left visible as per Gehna's instruction, added an authentic touch to his disguised appearance.

With deliberate slowness, Afzal lifted the hem of his T-shirt, pretending to adjust the waistband where his service gun rested. The polished metal glinted for a moment, catching the light and sending a silent message. The manager's polite smile stiffened, his eyes darting nervously between the gun and Afzal's inscrutable expression.

"Madam andar trial ke liye gai hui hai," Afzal stated, his voice low and calm, but with an edge sharp enough to silence any further questions. "Aaengi ghante bhar mein toh le jauunga." He adjusted himself in the driver's seat, shifting to find a more comfortable position, emphasizing his claim of patience.

"But sir—"

"Tab tak, mein aur yeh jeep yahin rahengi," Afzal cut him off, leaning back and crossing his arms over his chest. The look he gave the manager was unyielding, a silent dare.

The manager's throat bobbed as he swallowed. Panic sparked in his chest, not just for himself but for the safety of everyone in the building. "Mein aur yeh jeep," he repeated weakly, more to himself than to Afzal, trying to process the situation.

"Yahin rahengi," Afzal confirmed, his voice flat and final.

Desperation sharpened the manager's senses. He needed more information—for the safety of his staff and clients. Taking a breath to steady his nerves, he cleared his throat and asked, "Sir, can you share the name, please? I mean, your ma'am's name. Not yours."

Afzal's gaze flickered, but he offered no immediate answer. The silence stretched, charged and thick. The manager's fingers twitched by his sides, prepared for a response—any response—that would tell him whether to stay or run.

Afzal leaned forward, the leather seat creaking under him. His eyes narrowed further, and a thin smile ghosted his lips.

Afzal waved Upadhyay away from the jeep, his expression tight with tension. The plan was moving smoothly, and the manager's anxious glance confirmed it.

Inside the gym, the manager flipped through the register, eyes darting for any new entry. He found Kajal's name and looked up at the man behind the counter. "Where is she?" he asked, scanning the room. But she was nowhere in sight. Frustration tightened his jaw as he tried to mask any hint of concern. He needed to find her, offer her the best trainers, and make her a regular. But she had vanished.

Suddenly, a scream shattered the routine hum of the gym. "Aaahhhhh!" The sound came from a man collapsing onto the floor. The manager and a trainer rushed over to find someone sprawled out, clutching his right arm, eyes glazed and mouth struggling for words.

"Get him to the hospital," the manager ordered, but the room was frozen in shock. A woman, Gehna, pushed her way through the crowd. "I have a car outside," she said urgently. "I'll take him. There's a hospital just 200 meters away. Hurry!"

The manager and another man helped move the unconscious Abhinab, guiding him and Gehna to the waiting police jeep. The manager's eyes caught her for a split second before the urgency of the situation pulled him back.

"Get him in the back seat. I'll hold him," Gehna said, climbing in.

"I'll send someone with you," the manager offered.

"No need. We've got it," Gehna said as Afzal, behind the wheel, watched them get in. He sped away, leaving the manager and the helper standing outside, watching the jeep disappear, their faces lined with worry.

Inside the vehicle, Afzal checked the rear-view mirror. Gehna's gym clothes clung to her, yoga pants and a snug sweatshirt highlighting the sports bra underneath.

"You didn't look up, right?" he asked, eyes flicking between the road and her.

"No, I stayed in the blind spots," Gehna replied, slipping on a jacket.

"It's hot outside, what are you doing?" Afzal muttered, unable to take his eyes off her.

"Tujhe jhankiyan dikhane ke liye kapde nahin pehenti mein. Road par dhyan de," Gehna snapped as she zipped her jacket, glancing at the unconscious man beside her.

"When will he wake up?" she asked, tucking her legs up into the seat.

"Tomorrow. The drug will wear off in 8 to 10 hours. By then, we'll be home," Afzal said. It was still early afternoon, sunlight slanting through the trees.

"Waah," Gehna said, finding a cushion in the back and settling in.

"Take the front seat. You're making me look like a driver," Afzal called out, clearing the passenger side.

"I'm tired. I need sleep. Didn't get any last night," Gehna said, pulling a blanket over herself.

"Do I look like a driver? Come fill this seat so I don't drift off and kill us all," Afzal said, a playful command in his tone.

"First, I'm not your wife. Second, tujhe toh maathe par goli lagegi, accident mein marne vaalon mein nahin hai tu," she shot back, making him go quiet.

Gehna stayed alert, noticing Afzal stealing glances at her. Time passed slowly as they drove, with the occasional stop to stretch the journey. She couldn't afford to relax, not after everything that had happened. The toll gates were easy, but the real challenge was keeping her guard up. After a while, exhaustion pulled her under, and she dozed off, only to wake up to the noise of a crowded market.

"Why are we here?" she said, eyes wide as she took in the bustling scene.

"Your idea, remember? Getting food packed from the dhaba. And I'm dropping you and him behind the temple, our usual spot," Afzal replied.

"No, we need to change plans. Take the road heading into the forest, then the narrow path by the tubewell," she insisted.

"I'm not sticking around when he wakes up, Gehna. This beard itches, and I need to go."

"We had a deal," she reminded him sharply.

"I agreed to the kidnapping, not being your chauffeur," he retorted.

"Katai baddeemag ho liya hai tu, dono ko jail karawega. Get us out of here or we'll both end up in jail," she threatened, covering part of Abhinab's face with her dupatta to make him look asleep. Reluctantly, Afzal turned the jeep, steering it through the dense forest until they stopped in front of an old warehouse.

"Farmhouse. Nine o'clock," Afzal said, slipping on his sunglasses and tossing the food bags at her before driving off with a parting gesture.

Gehna pulled Abhinab inside, where Anand sat playing chess alone. "Good evening," she said, noting the dried-out pot and his weary eyes. She dropped Abhinab on a stack of hay and tossed food to Anand, who immediately tore into it.

"He's the sniper?" Gehna found another chain fastened to a metal hook on the wall. She dragged Abhinab by the leg to a different corner, securing him far enough from Anand so they couldn't reach each other or help in any way.

"What's next? What if he refuses?" Gehna asked, turning to Anand, who was already back at his chess game, taking a bite from a chapati roll stuffed with Aloo Gobhi. He glanced up at her.

"I'll take care of the convincing. But now we need a boxer and a runner."

"What about the route, cars, any other details? We can't just focus on people alone. How will we track them? Where will we intercept them? And what if they catch on to us?"

"That's why you hired—sorry, kidnapped—me," Anand said dryly.

"What?"

"To think. And I'd be more useful if I wasn't chained to the floor."

"Get back to work." Gehna sat back on the hay, casting a glance at Abhinab and then at her phone, leaving Anand to his food and chess.

"Who is he?" Anand asked, studying Abhinab to gauge how he could be useful.

"Abhinab Sindra, Olympic-level shooter."

"Oh, so you've kidnapped a legend."

"He's also a dead man walking, like you, if things go south." Gehna's phone buzzed with a notification, making her expression tighten. She stood up abruptly and left the room.

"I want his stats printed," Anand called out after her as the door closed. Whether she heard him or not, he couldn't tell.

Anand glanced at Abhinab, who lay face down in cow dung. "A rookie's in the house," he muttered, placing a black rook piece on the chessboard. Something about the situation felt off to Anand at first. The stakes were as high and intense as those in a movie, the kind that makes you grip your seat. Intelligence often came with boredom, dissecting situations and reading people, but these moments were strangely entertaining in their danger. Yet, a gnawing fear of death kept him on edge. He needed to cooperate with Gehna, ensuring she got what she needed to pull this off.

This was going to become perilous in the coming weeks, and Anand had to plan carefully to avoid casualties.

"Let's use what we have wisely," he thought, staring at the board.

—

Driving home, Gehna turned the wheel, the evening sky stretching out like a muted canvas. She needed to change into something comfortable—something that would cover every inch of her, shield her from the world, and hide the scars, both seen and unseen. The thought lingered, but it was one that never quite let go. Dresses, suits, and casual clothes—they were never about style, never about beauty. They were just things to blend in, to vanish in the crowd. But now, it felt different. These days, it felt like she was hiding from everyone, from everything, and even from herself. She did her best to remain unseen, to fade into the shadows, to escape notice. "You can always start over, a new life, a new place, but you can't outrun your past. You can't change the story, undo the things you've done, or erase the choices you've made. The consequences will follow you, no matter how far you run. But I'll deal with them when the time comes."

The tires crunched on the gravel as Gehna parked her car, the stillness of the evening disturbed by the loud call of her mother from the gate. "Kahan thi!" Her mother's voice rang out, sharp and filled with worry, as she sat waiting by the driveway.

"Kabse baithi hai yahan?" Gehna hurried out, taking her mother's hand to help her up. Her mother's brow furrowed with concern as she stood. "Tu thi kahan, bata, raat kat gayi, din badh gaya."

The words hit her harder than she expected. Gehna paused before stepping inside the house, swallowing the lump in her throat. "Tere baapu ne khana nahi khaya subah se. Police mein rapat likhne jaa rahe the," her mother continued.

Gehna turned to look at her, her throat thick with unspoken things. "I told him, I went to court to file some documents," she said. But her mind raced with another lie, another story to tell. "But don't tell me you were at the panchayat office, because you weren't. Where were you really?"

The question hung in the air, and for a moment, Gehna felt like she might crack open. The emotions pressed against her chest, but she held them back. If she allowed them to spill over, there would be no stopping the flood, no hiding from the truth. "I… I went to the district office," she said slowly, trying to sound steady. "I'm looking for funds for scholarships, for the kids' education. I announced it at the last panchayat meeting, and I need to get it done soon. It'll help us in the next elections." Her eyes met her mother's, trying not to look away, trying to convince her of the lie.

Her mother studied her for a long moment, then turned without another word. It was as if she understood, as if she knew better than to press further. Gehna followed her into the kitchen.

"If you're going to lie, don't tell me anything," her mother said, voice quiet but firm. "I'd rather be ignored than lied to."

"Maate! Are mein-" Gehna began, but her mother waved her off with a soft smile.

"I know, whatever you're doing, you're not bad," she said, her voice filled with quiet pride. "I've raised a strong daughter. And I can take pride in that. Just, take it easy for a while, okay? Rest. Eat something."

Gehna hadn't realized how long it had been since she'd had anything to eat or drink. She felt the ache in her stomach as her mother turned back to the stove.

"What's for dinner?" Gehna asked, her voice faint with hunger.

"Aloo Gobhi," her mother replied, smiling as she turned to look at her.

The words hit her like a wave, and for a moment, she froze. *Aloo Gobhi*. The dish her mother had always made with such care. But now, all she could think was Anand—sitting somewhere, eating Aloo Gobhi, while she was here, caught in a web of choices she couldn't undo. The weight of it all pressed down on her. She hadn't stopped to think about whether any of this was right, whether she was doing the right thing. But in that moment, there was no time for self-reflection. She needed to eat. She needed to breathe. Tomorrow was another day.

Her phone buzzed, and her eyes went to the screen. Afzal had sent a picture, one that made her stomach churn. Along with it, the message: *Aaja baith ja*. The reminder of everything she still had to do, everything she was tied to. Tomorrow morning, she quickly typed back.

Afzal replied almost instantly: *Abhi iska kya karun? Mujhe toh abhi chahiye. Ek ghanta hai tere paas, phir main vahan aaunga.*

Gehna's heart skipped a beat. She ignored the message for a moment, then stood up, feeling the weight of her decision as she pushed it to the back of her mind. Her family was fast asleep when she stepped outside, wrapping herself in a blanket, hiding her face, hiding her truth.

Her phone rang again. Afzal's name blinked on the screen, a reminder of what was waiting for her. With a frustrated sigh, she answered the call.

"Arre aa rahi hun, saale. Khada rakh. Aur call mat kariye," she snapped, her voice full of annoyance. She hung up without a second thought, throwing the phone on the passenger seat with disgust as she started the engine. The road ahead felt long, and yet, in this moment, it was the only path she could walk.

—

Entering the farmhouse, everything around her felt oddly still. The only movement was from the security guards, their eyes sharp and vigilant, scanning every vehicle, every figure that passed through the gate. “Salaam ma’am,” one of them greeted her, but Gehna barely acknowledged them. She didn’t want to be recognized, especially not here. The thoughts that crossed her mind were not ones she could ever speak aloud—the roles they might think she played in this place—mistress, prostitute, or worse still, a whore. It wasn’t that she cared about the judgments of strangers, but the thought that somewhere, someone might see her that way, it felt like a weight on her chest, a shame so sharp she could almost taste it.

The stress of it all had been building up, and now her body was paying the price. She felt an intense pain in her stomach as she walked further into the house, the ache too sudden to ignore. When she found Afzal, who was enjoying a glass of wine, but the moment his eyes met hers, his smile faltered. He instantly noticed something was wrong.

"Gehna!" He rushed to her side, his expression turning serious when he saw the blood staining her clothes, leaving a trail back to the door. "You’re on your period," he said, the words hanging between them. There was a flicker of frustration in his eyes, disappointment with his luck, the plans he had made falling apart. He hadn’t thought to check her cycle, hadn’t planned for this. But in the back of his mind, he thought, she knew.

Without another word, he guided her toward the bathroom, his hands steady as he turned on the geyser and tested the water temperature. “Take a bath. I’ll find you something to wear.” He left the room, his steps slow as he started to understand the toll all this was taking on her. He found a fresh set of clothes for her, then knocked softly on the bathroom door. “Are you okay?” he asked.

"Give me some time," Gehna's voice, soft and distant, told him everything he needed to know. Nothing was going to happen tonight.

She emerged later, finding Afzal seated at the dining table, frustration written all over his face. "Bistar laga hai chalo," he snapped, his temper rising. He wanted to believe it was all some sort of timing on her part, but how could anyone plan their period? His mind churned, but his desperation started to drown out the rational thoughts.

"Chutiya hai kya?" Gehna said, keeping her distance as she took a seat at the table. Her voice was calm, but her body was screaming for relief.

Afzal, still restless, couldn't hold back. He moved behind her, his hands slipping around her, touching her in ways that made her stomach twist in discomfort. She tried to resist, but the pain was unbearable, her focus scattered. She fell to the floor, crawling away from him, her voice weak but firm, "Nahin, abhi nahi."

"I know you want me. And it's not like I'm against it," she said softly, the words heavy with meaning. "I kinda liked it when you were rough with me. But please, thoda wait kar. I'm yours whenever you want." Her hands folded together on the table, and she lowered her head, exhaustion pulling her into herself.

Afzal's urgency softened as he listened. Something in his mind shifted, and he pulled back, his desire giving way to a reluctant understanding.

"Take me home," Gehna finally said, breaking the silence between them.

Afzal stood, helping her to her feet, and guided her toward his car. But Gehna stopped him, her voice firm. "No, not yours. My car. I don't want any misunderstandings with my family, or anyone seeing your car here this late."

Afzal hesitated, but then nodded, accepting her request. He walked her to her car, opening the passenger door for her. "I'll drop you off first and then have my driver pick me up."

Gehna didn't argue. She sank into the passenger seat, a warm water bag pressed to her stomach. The ache in her body matched the heaviness in her chest, but she didn't resist. Tonight, there was nothing left to fight.

—

Abhinab, waking up with his face lying in the cow dung and manure his realized hit the moment he sat backed against the wall focusing on the surroundings, with faded and blurry clarity,

"What the—? Where am I? Who chained me here? Anand? Is that you?" Abhinab focused on the figure and realized it's the grandmaster who had been missing. Groggy against the chains.

"Morning, Abhinab. You're sharper than your aim today." Anand calmly moved a rook on his portable chess board.

"Stop messing around! What's going on? Why am I chained? Did you do this?"

"Let's call it... a necessary inconvenience. Relax, you're not in any danger. At least, not if you play along."

"*Play along?* You've got to be kidding me. What is this, some twisted game of yours? Spit it out!" Abhinab began to climb over the wall, trying to sneak a peek form outside screaming out loud, from behind the walls. Anand doesn't react to his efforts because he was also desperate a while ago.

"You're here because somebody needs your help. And there's a... person of interest I need you to *help her kidnap.*"

"Kidnap? What are you talking about? I'm a shooter, not some criminal!" Abhinab smirked as he started pulling the chains and tried to scratch off the surface in which the hook was buried.

"Yes, a world-class shooter. That's exactly why I chose you. You have precision, patience, and nerves of steel. Qualities I require. Besides, *everyone* has a price, my friend. And please stop doing that. I've tried it, that's why I look like a mutilated toy. If you want yourself to be safe and sound, don't resist."

"*Price?* You think I'll just go along with some shady plan because you dangle a carrot in front of me?"

"*Shady?* Such a harsh word. Let me explain. Chess is all about strategy, seeing moves before your opponent does. Life isn't so different. We're in a situation. We're new in this but we have the leverage of being of use. We're shot dead if we don't perform well. And there's nothing you and I can do about it."

"And where do I come in?"

"You'll need to shoot. You're not killing anyone—just a little... demonstration of your skill. Enough to break into a few doors. He's the king; we're merely applying pressure on the pawns."

"You're insane. I'm not some thug for hire! Let me out of here, Anand!"

"Think about this, Abhinab. We're chained here because she already anticipated your reluctance. But here's your choice: help her, and not only do you walk out of here, but, actually that's all. You get to be free. But if you refuse... She will skin you, and then heal you. She's prepared and determined and you don't wanna make her mad." Abhinab looked carefully at Anand's scars, and the freshly closed wound on his forehead with the scars of something burnt against the middle of his forehead.

"*You're bluffing.* Someone's bound to notice I'm missing. They'll start looking for me. Not just me, they might be looking for us now."

"Oh, I've accounted for that. Your phone is sending 'all-is-well' messages to anyone who might worry. And this place? It's far from prying eyes. Face it, Abhinab—you've already lost the first few moves. Someone else is playing this game, and the best you can do is shoot." After hearing all this, Abhinab got a little tense looking around at the condition of Anand, in tattered clothes and polythene bags surrounding him like he's some sort of a rat, a domesticated animal. Trying to understand how he'd have survived in these scenarios.

"*...What's the job?*"

"That's the spirit. Let's just say... you'll be helping me put him in checkmate. And who better than a shooter to ensure precision under pressure? Welcome to the game, my friend." Anand smiled a little but he could see the hint of sympathy in Abhinab's eyes. But he had to play his role to get out of it, so what's the point of staying sad while doing it?

"Now when she comes over, say yes. We might have another company in a day or two, or maybe it'll be delivered today." Abhinab sat there in the corner with his stomach grumbling, and a dry throat.

"Please give me something to eat, and pass some water." Anand threw a couple chapatis wrapped in polybags.

"Just to get one thing clear, if you actually tried to escape. And if you actually did. Your family will be slid in pieces or chopped to frying bits. It's not something I was told, but I realized," Anand stared into Abhinab's eyes with his lips dried and a sense of hopelessness.

"And you don't want these words to be tried and tested."

Chapter - 7

THE HEAVYWEIGHT

"Who do you think would be the next, if there is a next" Abhinab asked, trying to fill the hollow barn.

"I don't need to think about that."

Holding on to a pawn in his other hand, Anand was having a game with just the bishop and the newly added rook, looking for the positions and the requirement in the game, while also going through images of the van, and the map.

"You do know something. You're here to plan this thing."

"I'm supposed to use what's there and make a healthy diet out of it. No meat, no bullets and no needless dying. That's my job, so please be quiet. I don't want to waste time leading to your death." Anand barely looked at Abhinab and turned back on his board, fidgeting with the pawn.

—

"The best chance is I bleed to death," Casually Gehna countered Afzal into agreeing to help her kidnap another person. Under normal circumstances, Afzal would be pissed and constantly look for opportunities to touch her inappropriately. But today, he was suspiciously calm. Probably the entire time while Gehna was with him, she was being rude and harsh with a dictation tone. She should've tried being more feminine to lure him, rather than dominating him. There's a visible difference: the person who's dominated will feel the immense pressure to fulfill the commands, pushed to do the acts and commit to things he or she might not be willing to do. But once lured, a person has a motivation, a kind of a situation where a guy gets a wish from a genie, it seems magical and romanticizing it is something which keeps the flow. The actions aren't forced, the motivation is a delusional state of mind and the push is gentle. And that's why it works.

"I can take care of it on my own."

Afzal and Gehna were driving into the dusty roads, crossing police stations and markets of different villages and intersections just looking for the Dhiwani, haryana village.

"I've figured it all out!"

With Gehna's silence throughout the entire hour of driving. Afzal finally had to talk about it.

"Anand, Chess grandmaster."

Gehna's eyes opened. She was just laying there with her eyes closed trying to ease up the moment where she didn't need to be concerned about anything. But hearing this name from Afzal was a little surprising. She did know that there will come a time where he'll understand and figure out the names, the identity of these people they were kidnapping. He's the superintendent of police so he was going to come across it.

The abduction of Anand could be understated as a personal motive, but with Abhinab's abduction, it has come to light that somebody targeted both of them, and the kidnappings are intentional.

"Aur Abhinab, Sindra, tujhe lag ke riya tha? Olympic level ke athlete uthaegi aur mujhe pata nahi chalega?"

"The timing is right. I was scared that you'd figure this out with the first one, but after the second kidnapping, this is pretty much what I expected." Ghena turned her head to Afzal, still laying on the seat, munching on chocolates.

"So, you're using me," Afzal pushed on the brakes too hard, drifting the car aside in the corner of the road facing the banana seller.

"Bhaiya, kele?" The vendor shouted and found the sudden rage in Afzal's eyes to be scary. He turned to see the police jeep and stepped away for a few minutes.

"Am I being used?"

"Yes." Gehna didn't need to be considerate anymore.

"Step out." Afzal didn't even look at her.

"You don't wanna know about my plan."

"Will you tell me?"

"Not everything, but I'll tell you your part in it." Gehna's voice was steady, her calm tone setting the rhythm of the tense conversation. Afzal sat silently, listening but choosing not to react.

"You called me. I wasn't looking for you; *you* called me. But I hated you at first—for what you did to my brother. I despised you. I wanted you dead, and just thinking about it brought me pain. Honestly, I would have loved it if you'd suffered." Afzal turned toward her, startled by her raw honesty. He never expected to hear this from her.

"I wanted revenge on you—the one who took the most important part of my family. The youngest, the heart of us all. I wasn't wrong to wish for your death." Her expression was blank, her eyes cold and distant as she spoke, unmoved by his presence.

"But then you left. You ripped my family apart and disappeared. Do you know what you left behind? A house drenched in death. That night, we mourned not just my brother but our own failures—our decisions, our negligence, our distance. We killed him with our indifference, but *you* pulled the trigger."

The jeep was thick with silence. Afzal, frozen and horrified, absorbed her words—resentment laced with years of guilt.

"Now that you are here, I want your help. I think this is the least you can do. And with our arrangement, I think you have your motivations cleared."

Afzal didn't dare move, barely breathing as he processed her words.

"When all this is over, I want you to do something for me. And then… we'll leave. Go far away. Just you and me." Gehna reclined in her seat, her gaze meeting Afzal's before drifting away again. "I'm yours to take anywhere. But don't question my motives. Just help me with this."

Afzal turned the key, and the engine growled to life, breaking the stillness. "How far are we?" he asked.

"Two kilometers," Gehna replied, her tone devoid of drama.

"So, who is he?" Afzal prodded, expecting details about their next target.

"He's a boxer. It's Tuesday—he's probably at the ring." Her answer was vague, but Afzal decided to trust her. He clung to the fragile promise of their escape, letting his mind wander to fantasies of distant beaches and her in dresses he couldn't yet afford.

"And after this?" he asked, trying to map the end of their twisted journey.

"We'll need a runner. Then, a private jet. To Goa."

Regret surged through Afzal. He'd hoped for a simple answer, not a logistical nightmare. But he swallowed his frustration. For now, there was a boxer to deal with.

Afzal reached for the bag in the back seat, pulling out a syringe filled with a sedative. "Fifty milliliters of this, and he'll be out cold."

Gehna frowned. "Why not use the cream? It's easier to carry and less obvious. A syringe could make him suspicious. What if he punches you and takes you down?"

"I'm not doing anything. You are." Afzal gestured toward a blood donation van parked near the gym, staffed with actors posing as medical volunteers. "That's our cover."

"That doesn't look fake at all," Gehna muttered sarcastically.

"It's not fake. You'll volunteer, convince the boxer to step inside, and sedate him. It's quiet, clean, and avoids a spectacle."

"Why do you always get the easy jobs?" she complained.

"Do you want a car chase? A shootout? Stop romanticizing this and stick to the plan," Afzal shot back.

"I'm not changing in the car." Gehna stretched and gave him a pointed look.

"I'm not a creep," he replied, a little defensively.

"You were naked at your farmhouse surrounded by men."

"I could've seduced any of them and walked away," Gehna quipped, brushing off the jab with a smirk.

Afzal rolled his eyes, gesturing toward the van. "No need to change. They'll give you a coat. No stethoscope—it's too much for the disguise."

By the time Afzal looked up, Gehna was already near the van, handing out pamphlets with her hair tied in a practical ponytail. A moment later, he spotted their target—Virender—leaving the gym.

"He's heading your way," Afzal texted. Gehna intercepted Virender, her charm on full display.

"Excuse me, sir, would you like to donate blood? It's for a critical emergency—a bus accident. Your donation could save a life."

Virender hesitated but started walking away.

"Isn't that Virender, the boxer?" a woman in the crowd exclaimed, pulling out her phone. Soon, others were recording, whispering, and pointing at him.

Cornered by his public image, Virender relented. "Okay, where do I sit?"

"Inside the van," Gehna replied smoothly, leading him in.

Virender lay down, still flashing smiles for the cameras outside. But as the sedative took effect, his consciousness began to fade. The van doors slammed shut.

"What happened?" Afzal asked, rushing over.

"Photos and videos—they're dangerous," Gehna said, concerned.

"Relax. Those are actors. Let's move."

Gehna was always surprised at how far he was willing to go for her. And yet, he never stopped wondering—if no one could stop you, what would you become?

—

With a resounding thud, the door flew open as Gehna stepped inside, dragging Virender Singh by his legs. He barely put up a fight, his limp form offering little resistance. Abhinav, already on edge, braced himself. He had been expecting someone terrifying, but when Gehna stepped in, dressed impeccably and exuding a striking, almost unsettling calm, he faltered.

For a moment, Abhinav thought of making a move to escape, but Anand's stories about her flashed through his mind. The way he'd described her—erratic, dangerous, someone who snapped under pressure—was enough to freeze Abhinav in place. He glanced at Anand, who was already watching him closely, measuring his every reaction.

The room fell into an eerie silence, broken only by the clinking of metal as Gehna moved about, gathering chains. Focused and methodical, she began fastening Virender to hooks spaced across the room. Each clink of the chains felt louder in the oppressive stillness. When she finished, she stepped back, locking the bindings with a practiced precision. Without a word, she turned toward the door.

"Wait—ma'am!" Anand's voice broke the silence, calling after her. "He wants to say something."

Gehna paused, her hand on the doorknob, and turned to face them. Her gaze flickered to Abhinav, who seemed hesitant, caught between fear and desperation.

"I'll help you," Abhinav said, his voice unsteady. "But... will I be free after that?"

Gehna considered him for a moment before giving the faintest nod, wiping sweat from her brow as she studied the scene. Her eyes settled briefly on Anand, her expression unreadable. She seemed to realize how carefully Anand had managed Abhinav, subtly guiding his submission.

Without a word, Gehna walked over to a corner and returned with a small bundle of food, neatly wrapped. She placed it in front of Abhinav.

"Khao," she instructed, her tone flat. Then, turning to the door again, she added, "I'll bring the last one in a couple of days. Stock your food, and don't eat it all at once."

And with that, she left, the heavy door creaking shut behind her.

The tension hung thick in the air, a palpable weight of distrust and desperation. "She brought a dead body," Abhinab muttered under his breath, bending to pick up a small pebble. With a flick of his wrist, he sent it spinning toward Virender's head, gauging whether the man was even alive.

"Should've seen yourself when you were brought in," Anand remarked, nonchalantly sliding his white pawn forward on the chessboard. His eyes flicked upward, locking on Abhinab with a pointed stare.

"What?" Abhinab squirmed under the intensity of the gaze. Was Anand actually staring at him or simply lost in thought? He needed clarity, a definitive answer to shake off the unease.

"How sharp is your aim, though?" Anand's tone was calm but probing, as if weighing Abhinab's worth. "It's been a while. But you're still practicing, right?"

The question wasn't idle. Anand's reliance on these men he'd plucked from their ordinary lives was precarious, their loyalty fragile. If they discovered his hand in their abduction, it would shatter whatever threadbare trust existed. They would turn on him without hesitation.

"I'm good enough for a couple of rounds," Abhinab replied evenly.

"But what if the target is hazy? Moving? Or… involved?" Anand's words carried an undercurrent of unease, his mind churning through contingencies.

"We'll cross that bridge when we get there," Abhinab snapped, his patience wearing thin. "And where the fuck is she?"

A groan interrupted their exchange, drawing their attention. "Bhenthot!" Virender cursed under his breath, his voice hoarse and broken. He struggled to rise, limbs trembling with effort. Slapping himself in the face, he tried to shake off the lingering numbness that made his jaw slack and unresponsive.

"Kaan u mein?" he slurred, eyes fluttering open to find Abhinab waving a hand in front of his face.

"What did he just say?" Abhinab turned to Anand, baffled.

"Kaauu mein?" Virender repeated weakly, collapsing back into the dirt. Dragging himself inch by inch, he found the nearest wall and leaned against it for support, his breath labored and uneven.

"You're somewhere. Kidnapped. Now calm down and drink some water," Anand said, tossing a water bottle toward him with casual indifference, his attention already back on the chessboard. "You talk like a toddler. Give it time."

Abhinab sat back, watching the composed strategist with a mix of admiration and frustration. Anand's calm bordered on maddening.

"They're definitely looking for us," Abhinab murmured.

"Yes," Anand agreed, not lifting his gaze. "But not in the right places. We're surrounded by forest and roads too remote for surveillance. Even if they send dogs to sniff us out, we're well beyond their reach."

"How do you know that?" Abhinab pressed, his suspicion evident. Virender, still regaining his faculties, listened in silence, his movements stiff and clumsy.

"Because I've tried," Anand admitted. His voice was devoid of hope, his words a bitter truth. "I've screamed. Cried. Shouted until my throat bled. Nobody's coming."

"I'll kill her first," Virender growled suddenly, yanking at the chain tethering him. It held firm, anchored deep into concrete far sturdier than sand.

Anand sighed, rubbing his temples. "Another one," he muttered, exasperated. "Look, I get it. You're angry. You were drugged. And it's obvious you're stronger than both of us put together."

Virender's chest heaved, but he paused, his rage checked by Anand's calculated calm.

"But anger won't solve this for you," Anand continued, his voice measured.

"Do you have a better plan?" Abhinab interjected.

"Yeah. Don't get shot in the forehead," Anand said dryly, meeting Abhinab's gaze with unwavering confidence. "If you want to try something, go ahead. All of us are replaceable. There are better shooters, better chess players, better boxers out there. In India alone."

"I'm the best there is," Virender shot back, wounded pride sparking defiance.

"Sure," Anand said flatly. "In your head."

That was all it took for Virender to lunge. Despite his weakened state, he pushed off with what strength he could muster, aiming for Anand. But the strategist sidestepped him with ease.

"Listen," Anand said, his tone softening. "We don't have to like each other. But she—whoever she is—seems to be calling the shots. And she wasn't working alone when any of us were taken."

Virender and Abhinab listened now, their anger tempered by curiosity.

"You both want to escape. I get it. But here's the deal: we help her with whatever she wants. Nobody dies, and everyone goes home."

"You're delusional!" Abhinab barked. "We saw her face. We're dead no matter what."

"No, you didn't," Anand countered, his eyes narrowing. "And that's why we'll live. The moment you let her face define your fate, you're done."

Abhinab hesitated, doubt creeping into his features. "I want to trust you, Anand, but this is insane."

"Look," Anand said, his voice laced with grim resolve. "I was taken in a police vehicle. Do you understand what that means? You can't trust the cops. If we escape and go to them, they'll kill us too. Just for trying."

He leaned back, his hands steady as he returned to the chessboard. "I've learned the hard way. If you want to take that risk, be my guest. I'm done trying to fight the inevitable."

Silence settled over the trio, the weight of Anand's words sinking in like stones in a dark, fathomless sea.

—

Chapter - 8

KAALA HORSE

Adding the pawn to the game, Anand turned the chessboard, taking turns to make his moves and adding an element of confusion and distraction for himself. "There's always an underlying move, which cannot be taken for granted, like something of a habit, a common thing with humans, which I can take advantage of," Anand kept talking to himself, as others tried to ignore him.

"He's delusional. And we're dying." Virender turned to Abhinab while Anand reflected an assured smile.

—

The television flickered with urgency, the anchor's voice cutting through the air like a knife.

"Breaking news: another athlete, Virender Singh—a boxer and former political candidate—has been abducted in broad daylight. Witnesses report that Singh left his gym at approximately 11 a.m. before appearing at a blood donation camp. Security footage reveals him enthusiastically participating, seemingly in high spirits. However, no footage shows him leaving the camp—or the van he arrived in. We now go live to our reporter outside the police station for updates."

Afzal leaned forward on the couch, stunned, as he reached for the remote to turn up the volume.

The screen transitioned to a scene outside a bustling police station. "Hello, this is *News All Over,*" the field reporter began. "Prashant, we have a significant development in the case of Virender Singh's abduction. The police have detained the nurses and the attending doctor present at the blood donation camp. We also have the police chief here for a statement. Sir, is this a case of hospital negligence? Or perhaps linked to organ trafficking?"

The police chief's expression turned stony. "Let me be clear. This is not organ trafficking until confirmed by us. Speculation is unhelpful." He adjusted his collar before continuing. "The nurses and doctor we apprehended? Actors. They were hired to stage the event. They genuinely believed they were part of a commercial shoot."

The gathered reporters exchanged bewildered glances. Sensing their confusion, the chief elaborated. "We are investigating further, but no one present at the camp seems to recall the exact circumstances of Virender's disappearance. Now, if you'll excuse me."

Afzal clicked the volume down, his hand trembling slightly as he dialed his phone. "Kitni der mein aari hai?" he barked, his tone edged with frustration and growing suspicion. For the first time, doubts about her crept into his mind. Why target athletes? And not just any athletes—national champions. It couldn't be about money. Her family's wealth rivaled royalty. Yet, his gut churned with unease.

"I'm outside," Gehna's voice came through, calm and steady. "Stepping in."

The moment Gehna entered, Afzal erupted, his anger boiling over. "What the fuck is this? You kidnapped three athletes. National ranking holders, no less. What are you playing at?" Before she could answer, his phone rang again. He answered briskly. "Yes, sir? Ji, sir. Understood." His expression hardened, and as he hung up, he hurled the phone against the wall with a sharp crack.

"Do you know who that was?" he snarled, pacing furiously. "The commissioner. He wants this area swept clean. Every. Single. Corner. What the hell have you dragged me into?"

Unfazed, Gehna lowered herself into a chair, crossing her legs with deliberate ease. "I didn't do anything. *We* did. And there's one more left."

Afzal's fist clenched. He hurled a glass against the wall, the shards scattering like his fraying composure. "Fuck off," he growled.

"We need to be in Goa by tomorrow morning," Gehna said simply, her tone devoid of urgency.

Afzal approached her slowly, a dangerous glint in his eye. But she remained seated, her calmness an impenetrable shield. Her gaze pierced him, unblinking, as if daring him to act.

"Agar beintaha chasak na lagi hoti na teri," he muttered through gritted teeth, "Maa kasam, yahin tile ke neeche daba deta." He spat the words, his fury palpable. "Pack your bags. I'm booking the tickets." He stormed off to the kitchen, leaving Gehna smirking in his wake.

She knew. She always knew he would fall in line. His ego, his resources, his very identity were all ensnared in her web. Afzal was a man blinded by his own desires, his judgment clouded by the allure of her manipulation.

When he returned, he found her still seated, staring blankly at the wall. "Who's the target this time?" he demanded.

Gehna didn't respond, only smiled—a slow, knowing curve of her lips that sent a chill down his spine. Her silence was maddening, her games an endless loop of frustration and intrigue.

"Still playing?" he asked with a bitter chuckle. He knew better than to press her. Asking was futile; forcing her was dangerous.

"What about my share of the deal?" he challenged. "You've got three samples already. Yet here I am, strung along like a fool. After this next one, I want what's mine."

"Fine," Gehna replied, standing up. She stepped closer, her movements sultry and deliberate. "I'm all yours, whenever you want." She leaned in, her voice dropping to a whisper. "But if a little blood on your precious ego sets you off, then take a breath." She trailed her fingers along his arm before pulling away.

"I've planned it all," she murmured, circling him like a predator sizing up its prey. "You'll be safe. I'll be free in a few days. And the ones we took? They'll all go home. Happy endings all around." She bent close, her lips brushing his cheek. "Then we can do whatever we want. Be whoever we want."

"We're leaving at eight," Afzal said, his voice heavy with resignation.

Gehna turned toward the door, her smirk unwavering. "Pick me up."

With that, she left, leaving Afzal standing alone, surrounded by shards of glass and unanswered questions.

—

The tension in the air was as thick as the dirt Virender flung at Anand, his frustration erupting like a volcano.

"*Chutiya hai kya?*" he bellowed, his hand hurling a clump of earth that crumbled midair before landing harmlessly at Anand's feet.

Anand, ever composed, brushed a speck off his shirt and met Virender's glare with an unflinching gaze. "That's your bit. You do that, and you're free. All of us are."

His words carried a measured calm, a stark contrast to the rage simmering in Virender. Anand's role in their predicament was one of delicate balance—herding strong-willed captives like cattle, each burdened with their own fractured egos and coping mechanisms. Keeping them united felt like spinning plates on a tightrope, every second a test of endurance.

Virender seethed, his anger an ever-burning fuel. Abhinav, on the other hand, was pliable yet skeptical, his suspicions about Anand's intentions growing by the hour. Abhinav's eyes darted between the two men now, his doubt a silent but palpable presence.

"I'm here to make it happen," Anand continued, his voice steady as he addressed both men. "To ensure that everything goes as she wants. Because—let's be honest—I want out of this mess as much as you do."

"I'll be out before that," Virender snapped, defiance sharpening his tone. He shifted restlessly, his chains rattling against the cement floor.

Anand tilted his head, a faint, rueful smile playing on his lips. "I'm sure you can win a fight in a ring. But this isn't a ring, Virender. You don't bring fists to a gunfight. That's suicide. Her bullets don't care how fast you punch; they'll reach you before you even raise a fist."

The logic hung in the air, heavy and unyielding, but Anand knew his words weren't enough to quell the fires of distrust. He needed this to go smoothly—not just for his sake, but for everyone's survival. Gehna's agreement to conceal his role in their abductions was the only thing protecting him from their wrath. It gave him room to navigate their volatile dynamics, but it was a fragile reprieve.

Anand leaned against the wall, arms crossed, and his calm demeanor unbroken. "We're in this together, like it or not. The sooner we act as a team, the sooner we get out. But if you think raw strength will save you here, you're as good as dead."

The silence that followed was a battlefield of unspoken thoughts, but Anand held his ground.

—

The hum of the airplane engines accompanied the weight of unspoken tension between Afzal and Gehna. Sliding a pair of forged identification cards across the smooth airport lounge table, Afzal's voice carried a measured tone.

"There won't be any need for identification," he murmured, eyes scanning the security checkpoint ahead. "But for safety's sake, here's our alibi."

The cards bore slightly altered names and photos, just enough to avoid scrutiny. Yet, as it turned out, the ruse was unnecessary. They passed through security effortlessly, their tickets the only requirement as they moved toward the gate and onto the aircraft.

Afzal, walking down the narrow aisle, typed a message to Gehna, his thumbs moving with the urgency of thoughts he couldn't say aloud amidst the crowded plane.

"Where will we find him?"

Gehna's reply came swiftly, "Agwada Beach, Goa. He's here for a vacation."

He frowned, his steps pausing momentarily before sending another question: "Wait, he's not Indian?"

"No."

Afzal glanced over his shoulder, catching sight of Gehna settling into a seat in a different section of the plane. Her eyes were already scanning the safety card in front of her, giving him no further acknowledgment.

His chest tightened as the implications sunk in.

"This is going too far," he muttered under his breath. "An international athlete? On diplomatic grounds?" He typed furiously, his nerves spilling onto the screen.

"This will escalate the stakes. Higher branches of investigation will get involved once it's out."

Gehna's reply came, curt and unbothered, "Will they find us?"

Afzal hesitated before replying, "No. But I'll need another cover if my name surfaces."

Her response was almost flippant, punctuated with a wink emoji, "I'll leave that to you."

Moments later, the steady rhythm of the flight resumed around them. An air hostess approached Gehna with a polite smile. "Excuse me, ma'am. Coffee or tea?"

"Chai," Gehna responded, reaching into her purse to retrieve a hundred-rupee note.

"It's complimentary, ma'am. No need to pay," the hostess assured her with a smile, leaving Gehna momentarily flustered as she tucked the note back and accepted the tea with a faint nod of thanks.

To her left, a man glanced at her, seizing the opportunity to strike up a conversation. "First time flying?" he asked with a casual grin.

Gehna's initial reaction was to dismiss him with a cold glare, but then she paused, her instincts nudging her toward a different approach. She pulled out her earphones and leaned slightly toward him.

"Yes," she said, her tone practiced, the lie slipping off her tongue effortlessly. "It's pretty overwhelming—being so far from home, stepping out of your comfort zone for the first time."

The man, oblivious to the fabrication, nodded sympathetically. "Are you heading there for work?" he asked, his gaze lingering just a little too long.

"No," Gehna replied, her voice steady, her facade polished. "I'm opening a bikini store, my first. I'll probably move there permanently, to take over the business. Technology isn't really my thing, so I figured it'd be easier to relocate."

She didn't flinch under the stranger's thinly veiled appraisal of her figure. She'd grown numb to such stares, her armor of detachment honed through countless similar encounters. Yet, for a moment, there was comfort in the anonymity of their exchange. This stranger would never know her name or the truth about her life, and in that fleeting interaction, she found a strange sort of freedom.

As the hours passed, they lapsed into silence. Gehna slipped in her earphones, shuffling through her limited playlist—folk songs and ragas interspersed with old Bollywood classics, looping endlessly to create a semblance of surprise.

By the time the plane began its descent, she had drifted into a light nap. The abrupt jolt of the landing gear woke her, and she straightened in her seat, smoothing her hair with practiced composure.

Both Gehna and Afzal moved quickly as they disembarked, their pace brisk and purposeful. They carried only small handbags, ensuring there'd be no trace left behind should authorities retrace their steps. In this game, caution was survival, and Gehna played her role with the precision of someone who had rehearsed it a thousand times before.

—-

The dim light filtering through the cracks in the warehouse walls did little to soften the tension that hung thick in the air. Virender's voice broke through the stillness, hoarse and commanding.

"Pass me the water," he barked at Abhinab, who sat cross-legged near a dusty pot and a cluster of muddy water bottles. To an outsider, the scene might have looked oddly pastoral, but here, in the desperate confines of captivity, Abhinab's position made him appear almost like a gatekeeper of resources—an arrangement orchestrated by Anand to create a delicate balance of power among the captives.

Abhinab raised a brow, the corners of his mouth twitching in restrained defiance. "Ask politely," he said, clutching the bottles as if they were treasures too precious to part with.

Anand, lounging nearby with his gaze fixed on the pale expanse of sky visible through the broken roof, interjected with an easy calm. "He's dehydrated. Don't make this harder than it needs to be."

The tone was measured, almost detached, but it carried enough weight to make Abhinab relent. He dipped the bottle into the pot, filling it with the murky liquid, and tossed it toward Virender, who caught it with a grimace.

"We've only got two bottles of water left," Abhinab warned, the words clipped with irritation. "Let's not waste it."

Virender drained the bottle in one long, defiant gulp, the water dribbling down his chin and streaking the dirt on his face. He hurled the empty bottle back toward Abhinab with a sneer. "Hagna hai mujhe, saale. Bacha ke rakhiyo."

Abhinab caught the bottle, his jaw tightening, but he said nothing.

Anand spoke up again, his voice calm and faintly admonishing. "We'll get water tomorrow, so be cautious. But don't forget to be generous."

Virender slumped down, his body radiating exhaustion. "I don't need a buddha preaching to me. I need water. And food."

Anand's reply was pragmatic, almost dismissive. "Sleep, and you won't feel hunger or thirst."

Grumbling under his breath, Virender lay flat on his back, glaring up at the ceiling. Within moments, his breathing evened out, the fatigue of the day pulling him swiftly into unconsciousness.

Anand allowed himself a faint smile as he tilted his head back and closed his eyes. In the silence that followed, the warehouse settled once more into its uneasy stillness.

The dim glow of neon lights bathed the bar in an otherworldly haze, the low hum of music punctuated by laughter and the occasional clink of glasses. Hussain was the center of it all, the life of the party.

"I can't, boys. I just can't!" he slurred, his voice loud and unsteady, a wide grin plastered across his face. "You got me drunk, now mishandle me as you like." With a dramatic stagger, he collapsed into the circle of women around him, their collective giggles echoing in the smoky air as they held him upright. The scene was chaos, but to Hussain, it was joy. The kind of joy that blurred edges and dulled reality.

In a shadowy corner of the room, Afzal sat nursing his mug of beer. His eyes lingered, not on the revelry but on a figure seated across from him. Gehna. The white sundress she wore was a work of art, embroidered with delicate lilies. The fabric clung to her body like a second skin, accentuating every curve and contour. It was impossible to look away, and Afzal didn't even try.

"That's him," Gehna said, her voice soft but firm as she gestured toward a figure across the bar.

Afzal turned, following her line of sight, and immediately understood. His gaze landed on the man she referred to—a sharp, charismatic presence exuding effortless charm even from a distance. "Hussain Balth?" he asked, recognizing the name before Gehna could reply.

"You can say, the fastest man alive," Gehna murmured, her words carrying a weight that wasn't lost on Afzal. She reached across the table, her fingers brushing his cheek as she cupped his face. "Now, what do you have for him?"

Afzal smirked, his hand trailing from her lips downward, a gesture as possessive as it was provocative. "You."

Gehna leaned back into her seat, the faintest hint of a smirk playing on her lips, but her eyes betrayed her apprehension. She swirled the beer in her mug absently, her thoughts wandering to memories she'd rather forget. "No matter how good you think I am," she said, her voice tinged with doubt, "there's always a bigger fish in the ocean."

"You'll be the best distraction," Afzal said, leaning forward, his tone heavy with conviction.

She hesitated. "You really think I can convince him to…" Her words trailed off, her uncertainty filling the space between them.

"Listen," Afzal interrupted, his voice a harsh whisper. "The police are on high alert right now. You can't fake an accident with someone like him. Not with everything that's going on. We need to get him alone, in closed rooms. That's the only way."

Gehna looked at him, suspicion flickering in her eyes. "What do you want me to do?"

Afzal grinned, the kind of grin that made her wary. "Wear a bikini," he said, the words landing with a weight that made her stomach churn.

"Is it necessary?" she asked, already bracing herself for the answer.

"Sati-saavitri se kaam nahi chalega," Afzal said bluntly, his tone laced with a mix of teasing and insistence. "Kamar, mumme, gaand—sab dikhana padega."

Gehna swallowed her reluctance, nodding slowly. "Theek hai," she said, her voice resigned.

They spent the next hour scouring stores for the perfect outfit, one that would turn heads and draw Hussain in like a moth to a flame. The experience was more uncomfortable than Gehna had anticipated, but she bit back her unease. Each piece she tried on was met with Afzal's scrutinizing gaze, his approval or dismissal guiding her choices.

By the end of it, Gehna stood before the mirror, dressed in a bikini that left little to the imagination. She didn't recognize the woman staring back at her, but she knew one thing—whatever doubts she had would have to wait. There was a game to play, and she was the pawn.

The tension in the air was thick as Gehna stepped out of the changing room, the knitted purple and white bikini hugging her curves perfectly. It was bold, even daring, and every inch of her discomfort was hidden behind the facade she'd learned to wear so well.

"*Yeh toh mein hi utaarunga,*" Afzal muttered, his eyes unabashedly raking over her figure.

Gehna turned on her heel, ignoring his comment as she prepared to head back into the changing room. But before she could step away, Afzal's hand shot out, gripping her wrist firmly.

"This is not the time or place," she said sharply, her eyes narrowing in warning.

Afzal smirked but released her wrist immediately. "Spicy," he quipped, his tone playful but with a hint of something darker beneath.

The hours passed as they prepared for the task ahead. By the time midnight rolled around, they had separated into different rooms. Afzal, who had harbored a strange fascination for Gehna, found himself repulsed when he glimpsed her changing her pads. The raw reality of it was too much for him, and he kept his distance after that.

"I'm just waiting for the week," he texted her, but the message remained unread, a ghost in the digital void.

When morning came, Gehna was ready. Clad in her bikini beneath a simple t-shirt and shorts, she met Afzal downstairs, her movements brisk and no-nonsense.

"I'm ready. Meet me downstairs in 10 minutes," she'd said earlier, her voice clipped with determination. Her mind was elsewhere—on Anand, Abhinab, and Virender, whom she had left behind. She trusted Anand to manage things in her absence, but the clock was ticking, and she couldn't afford any hiccups.

Afzal was waiting in an unregistered car, the number plates already swapped.

"When's our flight?" he asked as he drove, his eyes scanning the road ahead.

"In two hours," Gehna replied without looking at him. Her focus was on the task at hand.

As they approached the bar where Hussain was known to frequent, Afzal gave her the rundown. "You're supposed to seduce him and get him into this car. The rest, I'll handle."

Gehna glanced at him, her stomach churning, but she nodded.

Afzal parked the car strategically, not far from the bar but under the cover of a police siren to avoid towing. He motioned toward the entrance. "There. On your nose. Sitting at the bar. How hard is it to spot a Nigerian, baa baa black sheep."

Gehna gave him a cold look but didn't reply. She grabbed a water bottle, drenching her hair to add an air of careless allure before heading inside.

At the bar, Hussain noticed her immediately. His eyes widened as they traveled from her dripping hair to the curve of her body, clearly impressed. "Dayumm!" he exclaimed, leaning toward her. "Hey, have we met before?"

Gehna gave him a polite smile but didn't reply, her lack of English leaving her at a loss.

From his vantage point, Afzal swore under his breath and made his way over, understanding the situation immediately.

"Oh, here you are," Afzal said smoothly, nudging Gehna to sit back down. "There are no do-overs here," he muttered under his breath.

Afzal extended his hand toward Hussain. "Hey, I'm Aslam. And don't worry, I won't bomb this place."

Hussain laughed, the tension dissolving with the joke. "That was dark. Sorry, but I couldn't hold it."

"It's fine," Afzal replied easily. "This is my friend. She's not great with English—too much Russian and French family influence."

Hussain nodded, turning his attention back to Gehna. "She's beautiful. I was going to ask her out but wasn't sure if she was interested."

"She is," Afzal said, switching to Hindi. "Chhore ko ghani pasand aa gai hai tu, bol raha hai dinner ke liye."

Gehna hesitated but managed a smile, masking her unease.

After some small talk, Hussain asked, "Can I take her out for a ride? Just me and her."

Afzal hesitated, his ego bruised but ultimately gave his approval. "Fine. But take my car."

With that, Hussain led Gehna out, his arm casually draped around her waist.

Hours later, Afzal approached the car. Gehna was outside, her arms crossed, her face a storm of anger. Hussain was in the backseat, passed out and half-naked, his snores filling the air.

"Saale randi, samajh rakha hai kya? Kya bola tha tu isse? Kitne mein becha tha?" Gehna fumed, throwing empty beer bottles from the crate in the car.

Afzal dodged the flying bottles, holding his hands up in mock surrender. "I didn't do anything! Stop! I need the rest of those!"

He grabbed her arms, forcing her to stop. They both looked into the car, their task complete.

"We're done. Right?" he asked, his voice soft but steady. Gehna nodded, her expression unreadable.

——---

The dim light from a single hanging bulb illuminates the space, casting long, eerie shadows. The clanking of chains echoes through the cold air. Hussain stirred awake, his head throbbing, his muscles sore. His bare chest glistened with sweat as he blinked, trying to make sense of his surroundings.

Across the room, Vishwa, calm and composed as always, sat cross-legged, staring at the ground as though contemplating his next move on an invisible chessboard.

Nearby, Abhinab, lean and sharp-eyed, fiddled with a piece of scrap metal, as though testing its weight. Virender, his bulk casting a formidable shadow, lied flat on his back, his breathing heavy, and his chains clinking whenever he shifts.

Hussain jolted upright, his chains in his hands rattling loudly. "What the hell is this? Where am I?" His voice is sharp, panic laced with anger.

"You're awake," Vishwa said without looking up, his voice calm, almost welcoming.

"Who are you people? What the hell is going on?" Hussain struggled against the chains, testing their strength, his powerful frame straining as he pulls.

Virender chuckled darkly from his corner. "Good luck breaking those, mate. I've tried. I can't even smash them, and I'm a boxer."

"You'll waste your energy," Vishwa said, finally meeting Hussain's furious gaze.

"Energy? For what? What do you want from me?" Hussain snarled, his eyes darting between the men.

Vishwa sighed and leaned back against the wall. "You're here because we need you, Hussain."

"Need me? For what? This is kidnapping! I'm here for a vacation, man. This isn't right. You were definitely looking for someone else. That BITCH!"

"That Bitch! Did this, and she'll be here soon. But please, they're not mistaken and you're the right catch for this. So please let's not complicate this any further. We don't have time for a moral debate," Vishwa cut in, his tone suddenly sharp. "The only thing that matters is whether you want to get out of here alive and free."

Hussain paused, narrowing his eyes. "Go on. Convince me."

Vishwa stood slowly, the chain around his ankle scraping against the concrete. He gestured to the others.

"Each of us is here for a reason. Abhinab," Vishwa pointed to the shooter, "a sharpshooter who never misses. Well he's pretty much the best. Virender, a boxer who can knock out a bull." Shooting up his Ego, Vishnu carefully constructed the humour which was sensed by everyone but Virender.

"Damn right," Virender muttered, smirking.

"And me?" Vishwa spread his arms. "I'm the one who sees the moves no one else can. The strategist. The mind behind this little… gathering. "

Hussain snorted. "Cute. So what's your genius plan? Keep me chained up forever?"

"No. We didn't kidnap you, she did. And as far as I know, screaming, scratching the wall, breaking the chains, or digging the hooks out, I've tried it all, the only thing left to try is Morse code." Vishwa stepped closer, his voice lowering. "We're here to help her brother escape. And in doing so, we help ourselves."

Hussain frowned, suspicion flickering across his face. "What are you talking about?"

"It's simple," Vishwa said, his eyes locking with Hussain's. "Gehna's brother is in prison. We get him out, we're free to leave. And to do that, we need the best."

Hussain scoffed. "And you think I'm going to help you? Break the law? Are you insane? I'm not even a citizen you dumb fuck.

This isn't my problem. You're committing an international felony."

Vishwa stepped closer, his intensity rising. "You've already broken the law, Hussain. Or have you forgotten? That little doping scandal you thought you escaped? That's still hanging over your head."

Hussain's face darkened, his jaw tightening.

"That's right," Vishwa continued. "You're not as squeaky clean as you'd like people to think. Help us, and that woman ensures you walk out of this unscathed. No police. No scandals. Just freedom."

Hussain hesitated, his eyes darting between the other men. Abhinab watched silently, his sharp gaze like a hawk's. Virender stretched his muscular arms, cracking his neck.

"And if I say no?" Hussain asked, his voice low, threatening.

"Then you're shot dead, as someone else replaces you." Vishwa said simply. "And when the authorities find you, with drugs in your system and a bullet in your head, they won't be concerned about creating a scene."

Hussain glared at him, the reality of the situation sinking in. "This is insane."

"I'm really sorry for getting you involved in this, but it is what it is. It's already planned and you just have to run," Vishwa said, a faint smile playing on his lips. "Fast enough."

A long silence filled the room, broken only by the faint clanking of chains and the distant sound of dripping water. Finally, Hussain exhaled sharply, his shoulders slumping in reluctant defeat.

"What's the plan?" he asked, his voice resigned but firm.

Vishwa smiled, his mind already working through the next moves. "Good," he said. "Let's get started."

The warehouse door slammed open with a violent clang, the sound echoing across the cavernous space. Gehna strode in, her gaze sharp and unyielding, cutting through the dim light like a blade.

"So, how are we doing this?" Her voice, firm and laced with authority, silenced the murmurs of the chained men. All heads turned toward her. For Virender, this was the first time he'd laid eyes on her, and his confidence in his strength swelled as he rose to meet her. The heavy chains around his feet clanked, halting his advance.

"Ohh, madam!" Virender called out mockingly, his voice filled with bravado. "Idhar aaiye zara, ghana zor lagari hai. Mein dekhun tujhe, chaar chhore chain lagake heroine hori hai."

Gehna's expression darkened. With deliberate steps, she closed the distance between them. Before Virender could act on his bravado, reaching to grab her by the collar, her hand shot out with the precision of a striking cobra. She seized his wrist, twisted it with a practiced motion to its weakest angle, and drove him to the ground. Pinning him beneath her, she sat on his back, her weight a tangible reminder of his vulnerability.

Her voice dropped into a deadly register, cold and unwavering. "Now, if I see one more sign of deception, struggle, or any attempt at escape..." Her gaze swept across the room, lingering on each man before returning to the subdued Virender. "I'll put a bullet in you."

The room remained silent, save for Virender's strained breathing as he lay pressed against the cold floor. Gehna's voice softened, though her tone retained its edge. "I don't have any problem with starting over again, as many times as I want. But all of you don't have much choice in it. So act how your situation demands you to."

From the far corner, Hussain's voice cut through the tension, defiant and laced with sarcasm. "Hey, I don't think you understand, I'm..."

Gehna raised an eyebrow and turned to Vishwa, standing quietly at the side. “Vishwa, please translate.”

Vishwa, ever composed, relayed the message with the calm authority of a mediator, though the insolence in Hussain’s words didn’t escape him. Hussain, however, wasn’t ready to let it go.

“If you utter anything, other than LET’S DO IT! With a smile on your face, you’re dead here and now.” Vishwa’s voice shifted, cold and assertive, his patience wearing thin. “Including us. But if you won’t shut up with this ‘I want out,’ I’ll kill you first.”

The threat was enough to sober Hussain. His defiance faltered, and he muttered, “Let’s do it,” his tone laced with reluctant submission.

Gehna didn’t need to hear his words to understand his capitulation. The tension in the air had shifted, a silent acknowledgment of the boundaries she had firmly established. She exchanged a look with Vishwa, who nodded subtly. His ability to assert control over the group was evident, and she appreciated his effectiveness in fulfilling his role.

“So, we’re actually doing it?” one of the others asked, his voice betraying the faintest hint of doubt.

Gehna didn’t waver. “Yes. It sounds stupid, but that’s how it is. But you all have to trust me on this.” Her words were steady, commanding the room’s reluctant agreement.

Vishwa turned to the others, his calm demeanor anchoring the group. “Trust her. Trust us. This is how it needs to be.”

Nods of reluctant agreement followed.

“Good,” Gehna declared, her tone final. Without another word, she turned and exited the warehouse, leaving them to prepare for what lay ahead. “Tomorrow is the day.”

Chapter - 9

GET SET GO

The rusted gate of the jail cell groaned as it swung open. Deepak stood inside, drenched in sweat from his workout, searching for his shirt. Bhim Singh, the officer in charge of escorting him, leaned against the doorway with a smirk.

"Chal bhyi! Sasural se gaadi aa gai hai. Badi chaaku chhuriyan chalva raha hai bahar," Bhim Singh jeered.

Deepak smiled faintly, raising his wrists for the cuffs. "Aap nahin samjhoge," he said, the humor in his voice masking the tension in the air.

"Look to your right," Bhim Singh said flatly as he locked the cuffs around Deepak's wrists. Deepak obliged, glancing down the row of endless cells lining the corridor.

"Now, if you turn left, you'll see the same. There are many like you. Just circling around from jail to jail. There's nothing more for me to know or understand."

The clang of the cuffs echoed in the corridor as Bhim Singh led Deepak out. The air was alive with the jeers, cheers, and mocking sounds of the other prisoners.

"You've become quite popular," Bhim Singh muttered, nudging him to move faster. "In the wrong crowd."

Deepak kept his head down, ignoring the cacophony. His stoic expression didn't betray a single thought.

"Let's get you to a new house," Bhim Singh said as they approached a police van stationed at the gates. The vehicle was guarded by four officers: a driver, a co-passenger, and two armed men with rifles.

Deepak glanced at the rifles and chuckled. "Don't you think rifles are a pretty bad kind of weapon for close-range fighting?"

Bhim Singh snorted. "Jaa, try maarke dekh le."

"Buddhi kharab thodi hai meri," Deepak replied with a laugh. He climbed into the van, escorted by the armed personnel, who locked him into an internal cell.

Before shutting the door, Bhim Singh gave a final piece of advice. "You should back out. Don't get involved in anything. It's just five years."

Deepak turned, meeting his gaze with a small, knowing smile. "I know," he said simply, stepping inside as the officer locked the cell behind him.

The van's engine roared to life, and with a screech of tires, it pulled away from Bhondsi Jail, its sirens wailing through the city streets as it weaved through traffic.

—

As the warehouse emptied, the group's clumsy yet tense coordination unfolded in the fading daylight. Gehna, methodical and unflinching, unshackled Vishwa first. She pushed him into the cramped Maruti Omni, securing him in the driver's seat with a handcuff attaching his right wrist to the steering wheel.

"Is this necessary?" Vishwa grumbled, his tone a blend of irritation and disbelief.

"It's not like you're going to do anything other than talking and driving," Gehna replied flatly, closing the door with a definitive slam. "This will work."

Without waiting for a response, she turned back into the warehouse. Her voice cut through the shadows, commanding and brisk. "Chaabi kahan hai!" she demanded, ignoring any hesitation from the others. She headed to Virender, removing his chains at gunpoint, the barrel of her weapon a constant reminder of her authority.

"Move!" she barked, keeping her distance but maintaining her aim.

Virender, visibly annoyed but aware of the stakes, complied. He took the co-passenger seat in the Omni, his restrained movements revealing the unease he tried to mask.

"Where are we going?" he asked, trying to sound casual but unable to hide his curiosity.

"Hey, listen," Virender began again nervously, shifting in his seat as Gehna bound his legs to limit his movement further. "Is there any way we can get them—the police—out of jail one by one? So I can fight them? I mean, that's my part, right? Fighting them? But they might have guns..."

"Nobody gets to fight. If you fight, you die. Nobody fights anybody," Vishwa cut in, his tone weary but firm. He leaned back in his seat, rubbing his temples and closing his eyes, his exhaustion evident. "We'll do it quietly."

Virender squirmed under the weight of his restrained limbs and anxious thoughts. "Hmm, what if we can't do it how you want it to be done?" he asked cautiously.

"You just need to punch and get through. Just imagine your best shot and give it," Vishwa replied, his calm tone somehow unnerving. "I'm just asking for the best you can do. Chill, no stress."

The eerie silence that followed was broken by Gehna returning with Hussain. The tall sprinter surveyed the compact Omni skeptically. "I can't fit in this," he announced, disdain dripping from his words.

Virender, always eager to contribute, piped up, "Ghutne haath mein bharke baith re bhai."

Hussain turned to Vishwa with a furrowed brow. "What did he just say?"

Vishwa sighed. "He said to sit with your knees between your hands. Just try to fit in." He glanced toward Gehna, who handed him a folded map without a word.

Unfolding it, Vishwa examined the routes, his eyes darting between intersections, van checkpoints, and alternate paths. It was clear he was piecing together contingencies, though he muttered under his breath about the uncertainties of speed and timing.

"Where's the van?" Gehna's sharp voice cut through the cabin.

Vishwa glanced back at her briefly before responding. "Behind us."

The group turned to spot the **police van** in the rearview mirror, weaving through traffic with precise aggression.

"Rule number one," Vishwa announced without turning, "nobody looks directly at the van or the officers. Even if they're staring at you, ignore them. Enjoy the song."

He hit play on the stereo, and a slow, melancholy tune filled the Omni. The group exchanged uncertain glances before half-heartedly nodding their heads, clicking their fingers, and mimicking a carefree vibe as the police van overtook them.

"What now? We're here," Virender asked, his anxious energy bubbling to the surface.

Vishwa, who seemed to have all the answers, turned slightly in his seat. "We have two officers in the front. That means we can't try anything yet. They'll stop for a break. When they do, the front will clear, leaving the back section of the van with only the prisoner. Then we engage."

"And if they don't stop?" Abhinab asked, his tone laced with concern.

"They will," Vishwa replied confidently, eyes fixed on the road ahead. "They're lazy, and it's a long route. Hunger or boredom will get the better of them."

The Omni veered off the main road, heading onto a quieter village path. Gehna's voice rose from the back, sharp with suspicion. "Why are we leaving them?"

"We're wearing them out," Vishwa explained. "They're at their sharpest right now. Let them relax, get comfortable. Then we strike."

The tension in the cabin was palpable, each passenger lost in their thoughts. Hussain, bored and restless, broke the silence. "Why are we changing cars?"

The Omni slowed as they neared a small village temple, nestled between dense clusters of trees. Gehna, despite her usual composed demeanor, fidgeted slightly, the enormity of their task weighing on her.

"Haan," she muttered, acknowledging Vishwa's question about the second car's placement without elaborating.

As the Omni pulled to a stop near the temple, the group exchanged wary glances. This was only the beginning of a high-stakes, intricately timed plan. In the distance, the faint hum of the police van grew louder, signaling the approach of their first real challenge.

As the narrow dirt road wound around the banyan tree, the Maruti Omni came to a stop in an open field behind a temple. The Scorpio, sleek and shadowy, loomed beneath the thick canopy, its black windows an ominous promise of secrecy. Vishwa killed the engine and exhaled, his hands gripping the wheel.

"You're bound to feel suspicious of a car tailing you for 14 hours," he muttered, almost to himself. "And here we are."

Virender, restless and irritable, tugged futilely at the handcuff chaining him to the Omni's door. "Let's get cuffed in that car now," he announced with exaggerated cheer, the sound grating.

"Tham ja!" Gehna snapped, her voice slicing through the tension like a blade. She swung open the Omni's back door, her gun raised, the barrel shifting to cover one of the four men at any given moment. The message was clear: her control was absolute, and losing her grip now would cost everyone their lives.

One by one, they climbed into the Scorpio. The black screens on the windows lent an illusion of concealment, but the group knew the tinted glass would attract attention. Vishwa pulled the blinds off each window, muttering, "No use hiding in plain sight if we're begging to be stared at."

Hussain shifted uncomfortably, his lanky frame struggling to adjust in the cramped seat. "There's no way we can walk out of this careful, movement-sensitive bitch alive," he muttered, fishing for agreement. His eyes roamed the cabin, landing on each man for a moment before turning back to Gehna. "She's definitely going to kill us in the end. It's the only rational thing to do."

Gehna sat silent in the back, her face expressionless, her grip on the gun unwavering.

"See?" Hussain continued, now grinning at her mockingly. "She's not even denying it. We're going to die, boys. She doesn't understand me, but you do."

"What's he saying?" Gehna's sharp tone broke the brief camaraderie, her eyes narrowing as she caught the tail-end of Hussain's smug smile.

Hussain hesitated, his confidence faltering as his gaze met Vishwa's cold stare. "Shit," he muttered under his breath.

Vishwa cleared his throat, delivering a fabricated translation with practiced ease. "His daughter's birthday is tomorrow, and he needs to be there."

Gehna cocked her head slightly, studying Hussain before responding curtly, "He'll be free soon enough. Tell him."

Vishwa leaned slightly toward Hussain, his voice smooth and placating. "She said you'll be fine. You're our guest. You can leave tonight for your daughter's birthday."

Hussain muttered something unintelligible, slumping back in his seat, his rebellious energy momentarily dimmed. Virender, not fluent in English, stayed quiet, while Abhinab gazed out the window, oddly serene amid the mounting tension.

"The moment I get a chance, I'm out of this," he murmured under his breath.

Suddenly, a gunshot shattered the fragile calm. The bullet whizzed past Hussain's ear, the sound of shattering glass punctuating the stunned silence as it exited the car.

"This bitch!" Hussain roared, clutching his ear in reflex. "What the fuck is wrong with you? We're not even there yet! We can't do anything, so just chill out and sit in your seat!"

But Gehna's calm demeanor didn't waver. The gun remained steady in her hand, a silent warning. Hussain, his anger boiling over, kicked at the seat in front of him, his limbs jerking in a futile attempt to lash out.

"Bahot ho gaya tum logon ka," Gehna snapped, her voice sharp and commanding. "Ghanto se ghoom rahe hain, gol gol gol gol. Vishwa! Ab agar tune kuch nahi kiya na, maa kasam, bichha dungi sabki isi gaadi mein." Her gaze locked on Hussain. "Aur is kaaliye ko bol yeh jo bhi gol gol kar raha hai, na sab samajh aa raha hai mujhe."

The van they were pursuing came into view, its slow and steady momentum a stark contrast to the chaos brewing in the Scorpio. Vishwa's tone cut through the rising tension like a whip. "Everybody, be prepared. We're here."

He pointed ahead, the van gliding along the road just a few car lengths away. "He's alone in the back. Abhinab, your turn. Shoot the lock."

Vishwa adjusted the Scorpio's position, keeping its right side hidden from the van's windshield. Gehna handed Abhinab the Glock-17 with a suppressor, her own gun now pressed firmly to the back of his head.

"Do it," she ordered. "And match the sound with the hurdles on the highway. Wait until the van crosses the joint where the connecting roads meet. That'll mask the shot. Now!"

Abhinab's hands trembled as he slid the window down. Bracing his shoulder against the car's frame, he aimed and fired.

"Fuck!" he hissed, realizing he'd missed the lock by a hair.

Vishwa swerved the car, speeding up to create distance as the van moved ahead. Abhinab, pale and shaking, pulled himself back into his seat, avoiding Gehna's piercing gaze.

"Give me one more chance," he pleaded.

The cabin fell silent. Gehna took a deep drag from her beedi, leaning back against the door, her gun still in hand. The tension was suffocating as she suddenly reached forward, grabbing Abhinab by his hair and pointing the barrel between his eyes.

"I'm sorry! Please! Just one more chance, and I'll do it!"

"No, Gehna!" Vishwa's voice cracked through the rearview mirror. "We agreed—nobody dies. This isn't right. I'll get him out, just don't you dare use that gun for anything but a prop!"

Gehna exhaled slowly, her tone chillingly casual. "You'll be the last one, don't worry. We discussed this, right?"

The room froze as the weight of her words sank in.

"What does that mean?" Virender asked, his voice uneven as he turned to Vishwa.

"It means I die in the end," Vishwa replied with unsettling nonchalance. "But I still die, so no conspiracy for you."

Virender's frustration boiled over. "Tu bahut intelligent hai na, chhore? Chal, ye bata. Mein, Hussain bhai, Abhinab... Yeh hum teenon ke baare mein Gehna ko kisne bataya?"

Gehna's eyes met Vishwa's in the rearview mirror, and for a moment, silence spoke louder than words.

The Scorpio sped along the desolate highway, its interior thick with tension. Gehna sat back, the Glock resting against her knee, still pointed at Abhinab. The air felt like it could shatter with a word, but it was Vishwa's voice, measured and calm, that broke through.

"Gehna, I need him. We all need to stay alive to get your brother out of this. Remember?"

His eyes flicked to her in the rearview mirror, a steady gaze that said more than his words. Reluctantly, she shifted back in her seat, though the gun never wavered.

"I won't flinch again," Gehna muttered, her voice as sharp as her glare. "Or ask."

Vishwa nodded, keeping his focus on the road.

"And," Gehna continued, addressing the cabin with an edge that silenced every shuffle and breath, "it's not that hard to find your names on Google. If you're going to think, think about your dead body lying in the dirt."

Vishwa sighed, his patience wearing thin. "The only thing standing between that woman and the possibility of you all being dead is me," he snapped. His eyes landed on Virender, cutting him down before he could retort. "So help me out. And DO. NOT. MISS!"

He turned to Abhinab, his voice softer but no less commanding. "You can do this. Deep breaths. Just get it done."

The Scorpio hit another bump, the jolt shaking the cabin. Ahead, the police van continued its steady pace, the lone officer in the back visible through the rear windshield.

"Ambulance!" Vishwa shouted. The command snapped Virender into silence, his open mouth closing as Vishwa turned his focus to Abhinab.

"Ready?"

Abhinab nodded, his grip tightening on the Glock. He exhaled, calming his nerves as the van jolted over another road joint. The sights wavered for a second before steadying.

"This guy dies," Virender muttered darkly, his words carrying through the cabin in a sharp whisper.

Abhinab held his breath, aimed, and fired.

The lock popped off the van's rear door with a satisfying clatter, the small piece of metal tumbling onto the asphalt behind them.

"Re faad diya re, bhadiya chhore," Virender cheered, but the mood in the Scorpio was too tense to echo his enthusiasm. Realizing his mistake, he fell silent.

"Nice," Vishwa acknowledged. "Now, both of you—get ready."

With a quick motion, Vishwa pressed a button on the dashboard. Sirens wailed to life, echoing through the stretch of highway as the Scorpio sped past a line of cars. The sound jarred the sleepy traffic into pulling aside, clearing the path for their next move.

Hussain, sitting closest to the door, jolted upright.

"You're going to run," Vishwa instructed without looking back. "No fighting. Just run as fast as you can with this speaker. I'll play music to keep the distraction loud. Virender, you're going to get inside that van and get her brother out. Quietly."

"What?" Virender blurted, stunned by the casualness of Vishwa's plan. "Kya? Fir se boliye."

"You heard me." Vishwa's voice remained steady. "Hussain runs. Virender enters. We get him out."

Virender's face twisted with disbelief. "So I'm just going to jump out of a moving car, at 60 kilometers per hour, onto that van? Are you insane? This is suicide!"

"It's not a discussion," Vishwa shot back, his tone unyielding. "This is what we've got."

Virender snapped his head back toward Abhinab, his fury bubbling over. "He's definitely going to die, isn't he? Either way. Am I wrong?"

Abhinab said nothing, his shoulders hunched, his hands still shaking slightly from the shot he'd just taken.

Virender pointed a finger at him, his voice rising. "I'm not doing it. And if I don't make it, neither will you, *bhai.*"

"You are," Vishwa said simply, his voice cold and final.

The car fell into silence again, save for the wail of the sirens and the hum of the highway beneath them. Outside, the van continued its journey, oblivious to the chaos closing in.

The suffocating tension in the ambulance reached a breaking point as Gehna's lit beedi trailed smoke into Virender's panicked face. He turned back, trying to muster defiance despite the trembling in his voice.

"If you want to shoot me, do it," he challenged, gesturing out at the blur of passing cars and the van disappearing into the distance. "Because that'd be less painful."

"Stop!" Gehna barked, her voice cutting through the chaos.

Vishwa glanced at her in the rearview mirror, his grip on the steering wheel tightening. She met his gaze with a fiery glare that brooked no argument. Gritting his teeth, Vishwa swerved the ambulance to the side of the road.

Everyone braced themselves, the sound of gravel crunching beneath the tires filling the sudden silence. It was clear what was coming.

Abhinab tried to speak, his voice a trembling echo of fear. "We didn't sign up for this. I don't think you should—"

"You didn't sign up for *anything*," Gehna snapped, cutting him off as she stepped out of the vehicle. "You were taken in. No choice. Be useful, or be nothing."

Her beedi dangled precariously from her lips as she strode to the front passenger door. With a sharp tug, she yanked it open, glaring down at Virender.

"This is what we're going to do," she said coldly. "I shoot him, toss him onto the highway, and we move forward. They'll find his body in an hour—if that."

Virender gripped his seatbelt like a lifeline, panic washing over his face. "Vishwa! Do something!"

Vishwa, still cuffed to the steering wheel, was beyond exasperated. "Don't ask me for anything. I gave you a way. You can't expect me to babysit you now. This isn't a joke. I want to go home too!"

"Bhenchod, picture nahi chal rahi hai!" Virender shouted back, his desperation spilling over. "You're asking me to jump between moving cars like it is some action movie! Are you mad?"

"You're the most agile one here!" Vishwa countered, his voice rising. "If it was impossible, I wouldn't have asked."

Before Virender could retort, Gehna grabbed him by the arm and began pulling him out of the ambulance. Vishwa lunged for the door but jerked back, the cuffs rattling against his wrist. “Gehna! Stop! Don’t do this!”

But Gehna was unmoved. “He made his choice.”

She pointed her Pistol at Virender’s head. The helpless man sobbed, his voice barely audible as he whispered prayers. Everyone in the ambulance turned their heads, trying to distance themselves from the inevitable.

“Click!”

Virender opened his eyes, his sobs catching in his throat. Gehna stood over him, chuckling. “Oops! Main toh bhool hi gayi thi,” she teased.

Virender realized he’d wet himself, his pants damp with humiliation. Gehna casually loaded her Pistol, snapping the cylinder shut.

“Now,” she said, leveling the gun at him again.

“I’ll do it!” Virender screamed, tears streaming down his face.

Gehna smiled, yanked him up, and shoved him back into the passenger seat. His sobs were muffled now, his face streaked with sweat and despair.

“Let’s go,” she ordered.

Vishwa, saying nothing, started the engine. His expression was blank, a cold mask to hide the storm brewing inside.

“Where are they?” Gehna asked, lighting another beedi as she settled into the back.

“We’ve lost time,” Vishwa said evenly.

“Don’t you dare tell me it’s not happening,” Gehna snapped, flicking her match into Vishwa’s lap.

He slapped at the flame, a scowl darkening his face. Without a word, he yanked the wheel, steering the ambulance off the road and into a forest. The vehicle bounced violently, crashing through ditches and ripping through fields, the sound of crops snapping under the tires adding to the chaos.

Everyone braced themselves, the ambulance groaning under the strain. Gehna smirked as she took a drag from her beedi, the flickering ember glowing in the dim light.

Vishwa's silence was heavy, his rage palpable as he pushed the ambulance harder. It wasn't just the destruction of the fields or the rough ride—there was something in his mind, a plan brewing in the chaos.

Whatever he had planned, everyone could feel it was his last card to play. And nobody was ready for what came next.

The adrenaline in the air was palpable as the jeep roared down the underpass. Around the corner, they spotted the van—dust clouds kicking up behind it like an omen. "Let's sail for the climax," Vishwa said, stepping out of the jeep. But as he rushed toward the van, his foot slipped, and he stumbled forward, clutching the steering wheel for balance.

"Was that supposed to look cool?" Hussain chuckled.

"It was supposed to be," Gehna replied curtly, stepping out to pull everyone into the jeep.

Vishwa secured Abhinab in the co-passenger seat while Hussain adjusted the speaker strapped to his shoulder, preparing for his decoy run. "So, I just run alongside the van and keep them distracted?" Hussain asked, half-laughing, half-nervous.

"Yes," Vishwa confirmed, his tone serious as he tapped Virender on the shoulder. "Good luck."

Virender remained silent, the gravity of the plan bearing down on him. Sensing his hesitation, Vishwa pulled out a pair of iron knuckles. "You'll find another lock inside that van. Behind it is her brother. Use these."

Virender pocketed the knuckles, still saying nothing.

Vishwa continued his briefing. "The van will pass in a few minutes. Hussain, you'll run alongside it, leap, and engage them for 30 seconds. That's all we need. I know it's hard, but think of it as breaking a record—this time, for a good cause."

"Understood," Hussain nodded, stepping out of the jeep as the sound of the van's engine grew louder in the distance.

Vishwa shouted directions to both of them. "Hussain, run 50 meters ahead. The road gets dusty there—it's under construction. Use that as cover and make it fast!"

As the van came into view, Vishwa gave the signal. "Okay, boys, time to act!"

Hussain took off running, his pace matching the van as Vishwa tuned the speaker to blare a Bhojpuri song. The chaotic rhythm filled the air, amplifying the tension.

In the jeep, Abhinab raised a fist toward Virender. "You've got this, man. If anyone can pull this off, it's you. Wrap it up."

Vishwa handed Virender a mask. "This is for the dust and, well, just in case they spot you. Let's go!"

The jeep surged forward, closing the gap between them and the van. Virender climbed onto the side of the jeep, holding onto the metal poles for balance as dust whipped around him. "This is serious filmy hero shit," Abhinab muttered, eyes wide.

Virender moved with careful precision, inching along the jeep before leaping onto the van's rear. His boots caught the narrow metal stairs, and his hands latched onto the door's lock. The cloud of dust shrouded him from the guards' view, giving him the cover he needed.

Inside the jeep, Vishwa switched tracks on the speaker, ramping up the distraction while Hussain sprinted alongside the van, waving his arms and shouting nonsense to draw attention.

Virender took a deep breath, slipping on the iron knuckles. He smashed the lock with sharp, deliberate blows, timing his strikes with the van's jolts over the uneven road.

"It's been over 30 seconds," Abhinab muttered anxiously. Vishwa kept his eyes fixed on the van, gripping the wheel tightly.

"Come on," Vishwa whispered under his breath.

Finally, the lock fell away with a clang. Virender pushed the door open and slipped inside, greeted by the stale air and dim light of the van's interior.

There, chained to the wall, was Deepak—bruised but alive. Without hesitation, Virender scanned the chains, spotting a weak joint. He grabbed it and pulled with all his strength. The metal dug into his hands, but he didn't stop. Deepak, understanding his intent, grabbed the chain's other end, and together they wrenched it apart.

The sound of breaking metal was almost drowned out by Deepak's hoarse coughs.

"Oye!" a voice called from the driver's compartment. Virender froze, dropping to the floor and pressing himself against the side of the van, his heart hammering in his chest.

The sliding window to the driver's compartment opened, and a guard peered through. "Mujhe bhi aage le le bhai!" Deepak quipped between coughs, a smirk flickering across his battered face.

The guard chuckled, shaking his head. "Idiot," he muttered, sliding the window shut again.

Virender exhaled shakily, his mind racing. He turned to Deepak, signaling for silence. The next move was critical, and they had only seconds before the distraction wore off.

The tension in the air was palpable as the jeep screeched to a halt on the dusty road. "He's slowing down, shit!" Abhinab's voice cracked with fear, but Vishwa remained focused, his hands steady on the wheel.

"No, we'll be fine," Vishwa reassured him.

The van's back gate creaked open, and Vishwa hit the gas. Deepak leapt out, landing on the jeep with a thud. Virender followed, locking the gate behind him before making the jump.

"Nice!" Vishwa's grin stretched across his face as he helped Virender into the jeep. Abhinab grabbed hold of Deepak, pulling him in, and everyone settled back into place, their breaths heavy from the rush.

"You did it," Vishwa said, glancing at Virender, who slumped into his seat, sweat dripping from his brow. The jeep slowed as Vishwa caught sight of Hussain coughing by the roadside.

Deepak turned back to see a woman with her face partially obscured by a drape. Her eyes welled up as she gazed at him. "Gehna," he murmured.

Gehna pulled off the dupatta, tears streaming down her face. The sight of her brother—alive, bruised but safe—broke her composure, and she began sobbing quietly.

Deepak scanned the jeep, noticing the handcuffs binding the others. His eyes lingered on their faces, faintly familiar. "Wait, I know all of you," he said, piecing together their identities.

"Yeah, we're kind of a big deal," Vishwa quipped, steering the jeep onto a side road.

"Stop," Gehna commanded, her voice sharp.

"Can we at least get to a village nearby?" Vishwa asked cautiously.

"I said stop."

The jeep screeched to a halt. Virender's voice cracked as he pleaded, "We had a deal. You can't kill us now. We got your brother."

Gehna's face softened, and she handed Virender a set of keys. "As I promised."

Virender unlocked himself and Vishwa, laughing through his sobs. He hugged Vishwa tightly. "Thank you," he whispered.

The group climbed out of the jeep, stretching their limbs in relief. But their respite was short-lived. They turned to see Gehna and Deepak seated in the jeep. The engine roared to life.

"Shit! No," Virender shouted, starting toward her, but Vishwa held him back.

"You still want to go with her?" Vishwa asked.

Virender hesitated, then took a step back as the jeep sped away, dust trailing behind it.

Inside the jeep, Deepak glanced at his sister, who was smiling—a rare, genuine moment of happiness. "What's next?"

Gehna pulled out her phone and dialed a number. "Did you get it?" she asked before hanging up moments later. "Let's go home."

"Home?" Deepak's voice was tinged with disbelief.

"Yes, our home." Gehna turned the jeep at an intersection, heading toward the airport.

Deepak's heart raced as he processed her words. "Do you want me to leave the country?"

"No," Gehna replied, her voice calm yet firm.

Deepak's eyes widened as a familiar figure appeared in the distance. "Nandlal..." he whispered. His pace quickened as he stepped out of the jeep, tears forming in his eyes.

The reunion was overwhelming. Deepak embraced Nandlal, his emotions pouring out. Behind them, Sheela, their mother, looked on, her face lighting up with joy.

Sheela turned to Gehna, who stood by the jeep, her hands trembling. "Come," she gestured, inviting her daughter to join them.

Gehna hesitated, covering her face as fresh tears rolled down. She retreated into the jeep momentarily, composing herself before stepping out. Her steps were slow and deliberate as she moved toward her family.

But before the moment could fully unfold, a voice broke through the tension.

"You brought them," Afzal sneered, stepping forward.

Gehna turned, her expression hardening. "What do you want, Afzal?"

Afzal's smirk widened as he stepped closer. "I've done enough for you, Gehna. Now it's time to repay the favors."

"What are you talking about?" she snapped, pulling her hand away as he reached for her.

Afzal's demeanor darkened. "Don't play games with me. I want it now. You're not backing out this time."

Gehna's jaw clenched, and she stepped back, shielding her family with her presence. "Get out of here, Afzal. Now."

But Afzal's voice rose, dripping with venom. "You're going to pay your debt right here and now. In my car. Get in."

Gehna stood her ground, her hands balled into fists as her brother and family watched in stunned silence.

"Wait, let me just see my family off, I need to get the tickets and after the documentation, I'm coming back. Then we'll go, wherever you want. And we'll do whatever you want. Make a list," Afzal nodded, as he can't say no to one last wish.

Gehna took the bags with Deepak holding the rest as the family gets in the airport. Afzal waited, and soon enough he realized something.

"Bhenchod!"

As he saw a flight taking off.